CHRISTA WOLF

was born in Landsberg, Warthe in 1929. She studied German at Jena and Leipzig universities and has worked as an editor, lecturer, journalist and critic. She has written six novels: *Moskauer Novelle*, banned in East Germany and never published in the West; *The Quest for Christa T.*, which in the original German edition was allowed only a limited sale, *A Model Childhood*; *No Place On Earth*; *Cassandra: A Novel and Four Essays* and *Accident: A Day's News*, which won the Scholl Prize for Literature in West Germany, where the book was on the bestseller list for twenty-nine weeks.

Christa Wolf won the Heinrich Mann Prize in 1963, the National Prize in 1978, and the Georg-Büchner Prize in 1980. She is a member of the central committee of the East German Writers' Union and is a member of the International PEN. She lives in Berlin.

Virago publishes *A Model Childhood, Cassandra, The Quest for Christa T., Accident: A Day's News, What Remains and Other Stories* and *The Writer's Dimension*.

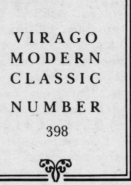

VIRAGO
MODERN
CLASSIC

NUMBER
398

Christa Wolf

No Place on Earth

Translated from the German by

JAN VAN HEURCK

Published by VIRAGO PRESS Limited 1995
20 Vauxhall Bridge Road, London SW1V 2SA

English translation first published in hardback in 1983 by Virago

Originally published in German under the title *Kein Ort, Nirgends*
© 1979 Aufbau Verlag, Berlin and Weimar.

A CIP catalogue record for this book is available from the British Library

Printed and bound in Great Britain
by Cox & Wyman Ltd, Reading, Berkshire

--··✦{ Contents }✦··--

I carry around a heart
the way a Northern land
carries within it the germ of a
semitropical fruit from the South.
It sprouts and sends forth shoots,
but it cannot grow ripe.

--◆{ Kleist }◆--

But for this reason I
fancy that I am seeing myself
lying in the coffin, and my
two selves stare at each
other in wonderment.

--◆{ Günderrode }◆--

No Place on Earth

THE wicked spoor left in time's wake as it flees us. You precursors, feet bleeding. Gazes without eyes, words that stem from no mouth. Shapes without bodies. Descended heavenward, separated in remote graves, resurrected again from the dead, still forgiving those who trespass against us, the sorrowful patience of angels or of Job.

And we, still greedy for the ashen taste of words.

Not yet mute as is suitable.

Say please, thank you.

Please. Thank you.

Centuries-old laughter. The echo, monstrous, bouncing

off innumerable barriers. And the suspicion that nothing more will happen but this reverberation. But only greatness justifies the trespass of the law and reconciles the guilty with himself.

A man, Kleist, afflicted with this overly acute sense of hearing, flees on the pretext of excuses he does not dare to see for what they are. Aimlessly, it seems, he sketches with his eccentric footprints the lacerated map of Europe. Happiness is the place where I am not.

The woman, Günderrode, banned by a spell to the confines of a narrow circle, reflective, clairvoyant, unassailed by the transitory, determined to live for immortality, to offer up the visible to the invisible.

The claim that they met: a legend that suits us. The town of Winkel, on the Rhine, we saw it ourselves. An appropriate spot.

June 1804.

Who is speaking?

White knuckles, hands which hurt, so they are mine. So I recognize you and command you to let go of what you cling to. What is it? Wood, a beautiful arc, the back of a chair. The gleaming seat cover of an indeterminate color, silvery blue. The shining mosaic of the parquet floor on which I am standing. People informally distributed over the space of the room, like the chairs, in decorative groupings. They understand the social graces, one must give them that. Unlike us Prussians. More sumptuous, more refined. Good taste, good taste. They call it civilization, I call it luxury. Be polite and keep quiet, it will be over soon.

It's settled, Kleist thinks, I'll go back this month. Just

keep calm. My feelings are of no concern to anyone, least of all myself. A witticism in which I should take some pride if I had invented it. When the opportunity presents itself I'll shock the poor Privy Councilor with it.

I obey him like a lamb; disagreeing with people is a pathological symptom. Am I able to travel? Oh, of course, I shall do what Dr. Wedekind wants. In God's name, and the Devil's, I'm a healthy man. Healthy like that fool on the rock, Prometheus. Who lives for a thousand years and then some. I'm itching to ask the doctor the location of this organ which keeps growing back, and whether he could not remove it from my body to vex the vultures. Now, now, one must not cozy up to the gods that way. The pious thing is to wish to be mortal.

Buffoonery. The little tricks of which the people here, in this bright region, know nothing. The fact that I cannot mingle with them, join the party. The invitation said: For tea and conversation. The wall behind me, good. This brightness. On the left the row of windows, the spacious view. A couple of rustic houses in the foreground, along the downsloping street. Tree-covered meadows. Then the Rhine, a sluggish river. And in the distance the sharp contour, the level arc of the chain of mountains. Above, the unwitting blue of the sky.

The young lady at the window is obstructing my view of the landscape.

Yes: the unconditional accuracy of nature. Fräulein Günderrode, hypersensitive to light, covers her eyes with her hand, steps behind the curtain. "Worthy is sorrow to lie at the heart of man, and to be your intimate friend, O

Nature!" For days now I haven't been able to get that line out of my head. The crazed poet. To seek consolation from a madman—as if I didn't know what that means. Already I am thinking that I ought to have stayed back at the convent, in the room filled with green twilight, on the narrow bed, warding off my headache, instead of driving here from Frankfurt in the maliciously jolting carriage, keeping quiet, refusing to spoil the mood of the others. Now they are leaving me alone, tolerating my remoteness, thinking it a caprice, and ask nothing more than that I exhibit my capriciousness from time to time. But, once and for all, I lack the inclination to dissemble or oblige others. I feel no urge to do anything which maintains the world. Its demands, its laws, its ends all seem to me perverted.

The pressure on her chest which she has felt ever since morning, ever since the dream which now is surfacing again. She was walking with a group of people in an infertile, gentle tract of country, at the same time alien and familiar, in her flowing white dress, between Savigny and Bettine. Suddenly Savigny raised a bow to his chest, drew the string, aimed the blunt arrow. Then at the edge of the woods she saw the doe. As always, the sound of horror she heard herself utter came too late, the arrow overtook it. The doe, struck in the throat, sank to the ground. At her side Bettine (she never took her eyes off her) was the first to notice the calamity. Lina! she cried, a lament. The wound was in her throat, she did not have to feel for it to know it was there. Bettine's white handkerchief turned red, so that Günderrode felt astonished at how bright colors are in dreams. Bleeding to death would have seemed to her so natural. Then from out of the ground before them rose a low canopy roof beneath which there stooped a gnome-like, shaggy being stirring a pot that contained a nauseating, steaming brew. And a hand—the only one which knew what to do—fearlessly dipped into the brew, which did not burn but was soothing, and stroked it on the wound in her throat. The magic worked instantly. She felt the wound close and disappear. She touched the spot as she was waking up: tender, inviolate skin. That is all I can have of him: the shadow of a dream. She forbade herself to cry and forgot the dream and the reason for her grief. Now she sees: it was Savigny's hand.

But why in the throat? That isn't the arrangement. She knows the place beneath her breast where she must drive home the dagger, a surgeon whom she jestingly asked about it showed her the spot, pressing it with his finger. Since then, whenever she concentrates, she feels the pressure and is instantly at peace. It will be easy and certain, she need only take care that she always have the weapon with her. If one thinks about anything long and often enough, it loses all its terror. Thoughts get worn out like coins which are passed from hand to hand, or like images that one calls to mind over and over. She is able, without flinching, to see her corpse lying anywhere she looks, even down there by the river, on the tongue of land beneath the willows on which her gaze rests. The only thing left to wish for is that the body might be found by a self-possessed stranger who will forget quickly. She knows herself, she knows people, she is resigned to being forgotten. Whenever possible, she avoids making gestures which attract attention. She has the misfortune to be passionate and proud, and therefore to be misjudged. So she holds herself in check with reins which cut into the flesh. It can be done, one can live that way. The danger is that she might get carried away, slacken the reins, and charge full spead ahead, and that then, at a wild gallop, she might collide with that opposition which others call reality and which they will accuse her of not having properly understood.

How fortunate that our thoughts do not dance in visible letters above our heads! If they did, any contact between human beings, even a harmless social gathering such as this, could easily become a convocation of murderers. Or we might learn to rise above ourselves, to gaze without hatred into the distorting mirrors which other people represent to us. And without feeling any impulse to shatter the mirrors. But she knows that we are not made that way.

Should a woman have such a look about her?

She makes Kleist uneasy. The young ladies of his Brandenburg homeland do not have this look; nor do the women of Dresden, attractive as he may find them; not to mention the Swiss girls—as far as he can judge by the one Swiss girl he knows. And the Parisian woman, who denies nature . . .

Is this woman beautiful?

An invisible circle is drawn around her on which one hesitates to trespass. It would be improper to bow or to greet her. She emanates a dignity and rejection inconsistent with her youth, just as her blue eyes stand in sharp contrast to her glossy black hair. As one looks at her, it's true, she becomes more beautiful, in her movements, in the play of her features. But is he a competent judge of the beauty of women? The mocking young Wieland often used to claim that women settle among themselves all questions involving their respective merits, and only ask men their opinion in order to flatter their vanity. If this is true, then the young woman at the window occupies a privileged station among the other young charmers, and none of them is disputing her claim to it. Certainly not Bettine, sister to the renowned Clemens Brentano, who, to Kleist's chagrin, retired with his young wife, Sophie Mereau, and another young couple, the Esenbecks, to a small table, immediately after their initial exchange of greetings. A caprice of which Bettine appears to disapprove strongly. She, little more than a child, unruly and unpredictable if one can believe the gossip, remains seated on the sofa with the two young Servière sisters, but her glances betray her: she would like to be at the window with her friend, but she does not dare to intrude on her unselfconscious obliviousness to her surroundings.

The young lady, whose name Kleist has forgotten after Wedekind's cursory introduction, is probably not very well off. Kleist recalls the unmarried daughters of destitute noble families in Brandenburg, the impoverished finery they put on to attend social gatherings, their flitting hungry eyes, their features already grown sharp. Ulrike, his sister. An unwelcome thought. Ulrike is quite another matter. Why? asks the other voice inside him, which he suppresses with iron discipline as he has trained himself to do. He pounced on that lesson and devoured it like a wild beast. This is the only way to learn: with one's life at stake, in mortal dread. In the thrall of Powers which leave no doubt about their ability to annihilate us, because something in ourselves which we do not want to recognize comes forward to greet and connive with them. This breakdown in November. The hideous winter. These rumbling, never-ending monologues inside his poor head. He knows what would save him: to gag the voice inside him that inflames and mocks and drives him on, toward the galled, sore places. And what if he could silence it? Another species of death. But whence does he derive the self-assurance, the conviction of his obligation to wrest their names from those Powers, washed with all waters, even with blood? And what, at the same time, is the source of his sense of impotence, and the pervasive doubt of his vocation? The two opponents are not evenly matched.

Kleist utters a sound which would arouse awe or dread if one could regard it as a form of laughter.

Someone touches his arm. Wedekind, the physician, practicing his profession.

May one inquire what has carried you away from us?

He is not the master of the thing inside him which thinks. He must restrain himself, and he will qualify as cured when he has mastered this art. But how can a man be cured who deranges the law before he has a chance to submit to it? Abases himself to the dust and submits: to the deranged, invalid law.

And of this law there is no judge. No judge.

Kleist, in affliction, shakes his head violently.

Kleist! he hears the doctor say.

Nothing, nothing. It's nothing. I was just thinking that this year I'm going to be twenty-seven.

To be sure, Wedekind says. And does that mean something?

An excellent question. The answer is: No.

Lethal benefaction: to believe what one says and to be torn apart by this belief. As for your friends, they always believe you least when you come closest to speaking the truth. Like that time long ago, last autumn, with Pfuel in Paris, who shared his quarters with him but not his despair. Pfuel, I'm done for! God knows it was the truth, but this friend who knew him best, who had been his companion, one might even say his disciple; who had witnessed at his side his doomed struggle to write the accursed *Guiscard*: this friend disputed his right to draw the logical conclusion from this truth, and denied him the benefaction of abandoning the world with him forever. He had not yet reached the point, Pfuel had said, of being prepared to dispatch himself into the Beyond; but he would be certain to let his friend Kleist know in due season if he changed his mind . . .

Privy Councilor, Kleist asks, you are familiar with *Hamlet*?

To be sure, the other replies. (It is his favorite phrase.) In the original and in the Schlegel translation.

A man of culture.

It has just occurred to him, Kleist says: that quarrel in

Paris which had created the breach between him and his friend Pfuel—he knew the one? Wedekind nods: the quarrel had been about the soliloquy. "For who would bear the whips and scorns of time . . ."

". . . The oppressor's wrong, the proud man's contumely . . ." Yes, no doubt about it, the Privy Councilor has been keeping up. But he cannot refrain from voicing his dismay that two friends, two civilized adults, should be capable of ending up at daggers drawn over a couple of lines of verse. Was this not carrying reverence for literature a little too far? Indeed, was it not impermissible to breach that wall which has been erected between literary fantasies and the actualities of the world?

Exactly what Pfuel had said. That *was* the breach.

Your eternal penchant for the absolute, Kleist . . . Did you ever consider the possibility that your Shakespeare may have been a man of infinite jest—that he may in fact have gotten a lot of fun out of life?

It crosses Kleist's mind that the physician considers him an actor who does variant interpretations of the same role —among them the tragic. If this is true, he does not choose to know it. He is dependent on the judgment of others and cannot do anything about it.

Other people want thoughts that are not drenched in blood. Harmony, moderation, extenuation. No matter how inordinate his exertions, Kleist is unable to penetrate to the interior life of words. Wasted by longing, I move in the reflection of their splendor.

Ready for print, he says to Wedekind, who waits for what will come next. Sentences ready for print, Privy

Councilor: it is a blasphemy. Each of them forged fine and sharp to guillotine the one that came before it.

Kleist, says Wedekind, if only you would believe me: it is not good for a man to gaze too deeply inside himself.

Thanks for the good intentions. If I had sunk so low as to need consolation, to accept the extenuating judgment. Keep a devilish sharp lookout now; I must make certain that I do not take my head between my hands and squeeze it hard, in front of all these people. What a beautiful assembly room. What charming people. What quintessential patterns they form, in unison with rules which I shall never learn or comprehend. My God.

Herr von Kleist.

Fräulein.

What is it that has made the color rise to her cheeks that way? Oh yes, of course: the arrival of new guests to whom she wishes to introduce him. Now then, what have we here? A Herr von Savigny from Marburg, a scholar of the law, and his wife Gunda, née Brentano. The Brentanos appear to be a prolific clan. This man Savigny, scarcely older than himself but, so it would appear, possessing a self-assurance which must always remain beyond Kleist's reach. Look how he holds the Fräulein's hand, how he gazes at her, knows to speak to her, maintaining just the right note—a cross between salutation, inquiry, and entreaty: Günderrödchen—Günderrode my pet.

Now he knows her name. Which he has never heard before. Without bestowing on him a second glance, she moves off toward the others, locked arm in arm with the two new arrivals. That crack in the curtain which had opened for a moment as if to admit him into her world is closed. This Fräulein Günderrode has approached him only to withdraw again. It is unjust to transfer to her the burden of his disappointment. Very well then, he will be unjust.

The light! someone says. Karoline, you *must* see it!

Clemens. How well I know him. Know that he cannot bear to see me anywhere near Savigny. That he is hauling me to the window as if I were his property, is extorting from me some comment on the lighting effect, which, as I already know quite well, is in fact beyond compare at this hour, when the sun stands at a certain angle in relation to the landscape and the reflecting mirror of the water. As if any phenomenon of nature had need of our praise, our devoted attention, or even our presence.

You are hard on me, Karoline.

Wounded ego, always the same old thing. As Clemens was dragging me away, Savigny signaled to me with his finger. He has come. He knows that I am waiting and counts on my being able to conceal it. He understands that when I love I am constant and selfless, and takes advantage of the fact, and I in turn must love him all the more. This, too, he has taken into account. And so it goes, on and on.

Savigny's entrance has afforded Günderrode a moment of joyous self-obliviousness, a quickened pulse, involuntary gestures which she is unable to control, although in all other circumstances she can govern and subdue every impulse, every upwelling of emotion, as long as she is conscious of who she is. Always the elder in every relationship, the mainstay of her widowed, impetuous, somewhat addle-pated mother, and responsible for bringing up her younger sisters; forever sensible, forever prudent, poised between the two contradictory poles of a spirit which was by nature soaring, and living conditions of the most restrictive kind. Those first nights in the convent, at the age of nineteen, on the hard narrow bed in the small room with the open windows, through which, when the last of the night birds had gone mute, there shouldered its way a silence which grew ever more dense, more threatening, and more final, and before morning seemed to fill up and to suffocate the entire universe. She never speaks of all this, and she does not forget it. Bettine, fond as she is of her, will never for so much as a moment divine what pain, what renunciation her friend has resolutely locked inside her.

Clemens likes to hear himself talk.

Kleist looks in their direction.

The group from which that Fräulein Günderrode has detached herself is falling apart as if it had lost its inner cohesion, and its various members are attaching themselves to other groups. Two or three gentlemen are gathering around Bettine at the clavichord. She strikes an arbitrary series of notes unrecorded on any sheet of music. She cannot sight-read, he hears her say, and she laughs so that he wonders: Ought he to be irritated by her fantastical behavior, or should he simply accept it, as it appears to be part of her nature? Admittedly he prefers women who remain inconspicuously in the background, like this Gunda, this Lisette, Savigny's and Esenbeck's wives, who have seated themselves on the narrow couch directly beneath the big oil painting which, by the most scrupulous treatment of all the gradations of green, has conferred on a simple landscape an incredible articulation, brilliance, and depth. A curious notion: a second painter, should he see the canvas, could apply himself to fashioning a second painting based on this new theme—the image of the first picture, with the little couch and the very dissimilar young women sitting there—designed to hang above the gentle arc of the chest of drawers on the narrow side of the room opposite him, thus forming yet another group which in its turn might serve as a suitable subject for a painting. In this way the process would go on and on, and would also introduce a certain forward movement into the art of painting.

Wedekind wishes to know whether his claims were exaggerated.

What is he referring to? The landscape? The people?

After all, Kleist says with circumspection, I was already familiar with the Rhineland.

To be sure: as a soldier. That is quite another matter. No one really knows a region which he has merely flitted through, wearing his regimentals.

Kleist cannot dispute this point. He shrinks from speaking to this native of Mainz about the time when, at the age of fifteen, as an ensign of the King of Prussia, he had participated in the siege of Wedekind's town. That was eleven years ago and happened in another lifetime. The memory of it would have vanished utterly had he not enclosed it in a fortress of words, which now enables him to conjure up the experience as often as he chooses: how he mounted with his face toward the evening wind and toward the Rhine, with the waves of the air and those of the water simultaneously resounding about him so that he was able to hear a fusing adagio with all its melodic phrasings and an entire harmonic accompaniment.

It was thus—faithfully, he dares hope—that he described the experience, much later, in a letter to Wilhelmine von Zenge, and he was well aware that the passion which swept him away then was the seduction of words far more than the need to communicate with any particular human being; for without thinking twice about it he uses the very same turns of phrase in letters to all sorts of other people, so that, as he himself clearly feels, he fails to confer on any of them the ultimate intimacy. Even when he reproached his betrothed for her lack of love, he was in perfect control of everything: the laments, the accusations, every single stroke of the pen. As he could not alter the situation, she ought to have put up with it, even if this was really asking too much. He can easily imagine, down to every individual turn of phrase, what tattle the members of Frankfurt society are telling behind his back. To stall his fiancée, and then to jilt her. Why does it matter to him what they say? Why this horror at standing up to their judgment? Why, when putting this distance between himself and them has failed to bring any relief, does he still feel the temptation: it is better to die than face that.

Ah: because their reproach confirms his own self-reproaches. Immorality! They do not know the meaning of the word. But he knows. To fail to pay life the debt it demands, and pay the living what they are compelled to demand; to feel truly alive only when one is writing . . . These ghastly six months in Wedekind's home. In some secret sense they had been for him an indescribable holiday: his condition forbade him even so much as to think about writing. In the nearness to death this compulsion to write falls away. One lives simply in order to live. Now, how could that idea be expressed?

You really ought to think about something else.

Privy Councilor Wedekind knows. When his patient becomes thus self-absorbed, it is time to distract his attention. He wants, he says, to hear what Kleist thinks about this gathering.

Oh, that. Quite pleasant, really, isn't it? Very pleasant, indeed. The only thing which disturbs him: in case the opportunity should arise, he would not know how to address that woman over there.

What's that you say? Careful now, don't show any surprise: Wedekind will be on his guard. It all has to do with Günderrode, with whom Kleist appears to be preoccupied. Easy to help the man. Given the fact that the young lady—who, by the way, albeit under a pseudonym, has just created a stir as a poet—is unmarried and of noble family, the correct way to address her would be Fräulein, or, if that would not do, Demoiselle.

All the same, the matter would give him some difficulty, it's hard to say just why. "Fräulein" seems to him in some way unsuitable. He cannot dispose of something for which he cannot find the proper word. Naturally, as often as expediency allows, Bettine calls to Lina to come over to her, while the latter listens attentively but without any real responsiveness to Clemens, who standing there beside her assumes the guise of a suppliant. The other young women call her Karoline. But this, too, would be an inappropriate form of address for him to use. Obviously, less appropriate still would be Savigny's term of endearment, which appears to give Günderrode unwarranted pleasure: Günderrode my pet.

The way she stands there, not imposing herself, not expressly withdrawing. Highborn lady. Girl. Female. Woman. All designations glide away from her again. Virgin: absurd, even insulting; later I'll think why. Youth-maiden. Curious notion; enough of that.

Kleist suppresses the word which seems to him suitable. He does not inquire into the roots of his antipathy to the hermaphroditic. She writes poetry? Disastrous. Is she compelled to do so? Does she know no better way to pass the time, to dispel boredom?

Günderrode feels the gaze between her shoulder blades and shakes it off. The stranger whom Wedekind has introduced to their group is standing stiff as a ramrod, not stirring from his spot, all alone. Someone really must take an interest in him. Why had Merten, on other occasions always an impeccable host, been negligent in his duties on this occasion? There he stands applauding Bettine, cannot take his eyes off her, letting himself be led around by the nose as if he were not a man in his mid-forties, a stout, sedate merchant, whereas Bettine is a slip of a thing barely twenty years old—the silly fool. If only he knew how, later on, she will make fun of him when she talks with me, refusing to listen to my reproaches, denying all responsibility. Everyone has to pay the piper for acting the fool, she will say, and after all, the same thing applies to her. She is certainly right there. In any case, what does this unknown guest in the house of strangers have to do with me? Perhaps later an opportunity will arise for me to let this man Kleist know that I have read his play. I have yet to meet the author who did not brighten up on the spot the moment someone he meets confesses to having read his work.

But on no account must she tell him that it was Merten himself who gave her Kleist's drama to read, and that, moreover, Merten was disappointed by it, as the title, *The House of Schroffenstein*, had led him to hope that it would be an ordinary drama of chivalry. Nor must she let him know that she had read it because of the singular rumors emanating from Mainz, concerning this young man who, in a truly wretched state, had taken refuge for the winter in the home of Privy Councilor Wedekind. In any case, one could scarcely credit this man, with his childlike face, with having depicted the emotional tumults or the savage crimes with which his drama was positively teeming. In fact, he is still very young.

She has to smile at that. She herself is even younger than he.

Now the sun is at the same elevation as the four windows, all of which open to the southwest. A current of air wafts in, so tenuous that Günderrode can scarcely breathe it. Often, when she is lying on her bed short of breath, she reflects that she needs twice as much air as other people, as if her body were using up an extra supply to carry out some hidden purpose.

A clock on the wall strikes three swift strokes, with the delicate and brittle sound of a spinet. That is no reason for this sudden feeling of bleakness. She has been here for half an hour, and already she would like to leave; she feels the mounting chill which normally accompanies this compulsion to flee. She wants to get rid of Clemens, whom she is finding irksome. He does not sense which things he ought to keep silent about; and she, shackled by an old regard for his feelings and incapable of touching on that incident that happened between them three years ago, must let him have his say. She feels the skin of her face grow taut so that it may become impermeable to his glances, which palpate her mouth, forehead, cheeks. She finds it intolerable that a man can take such liberties with a woman simply as a matter of course, and that she cannot defend herself against his importunity without, in the end, appearing prim, prudish, and unwomanly.

So, they'll talk about her poems, since he insists on it. She does not want to talk about them, does not want to reveal to anyone, least of all to him, that she is hurt, humiliated, indeed broken in spirit. So she tells him that she has never regretted releasing her poems to the public, thus casually, not knowing what she was doing, over-coming the barrier which segregated her innermost soul from the world. Not Clemens, not anyone should hear from her how deeply it wounded her that an evil idiot chance should have revealed the identity of the person concealed behind the pseudonym of the poet Tian.

But the review in *Der Freimüthige*? Was she trying to deceive him into thinking that that review had not hurt her?

Hurt? My God. Anyone who gives himself into the power of the public . . .

The critic is a fellow countryman of hers, is he not, a native of Frankfurt?

Yes, indeed. Moreover, some high muckamuck or private tutor attached to a noble household who signs his name with nothing but an "E."

A captious critic attached to a noble household! Clemens has heard that this man failed to make a success with his own poetry and that, insofar as he is able, he revenges himself on any artist of genuine talent who lacks the protection of powerful patrons. Surely, he says, she must realize that envy is a motivation of inconceivable power.

As for that, Günderrode cannot see that this insight improves the situation in the slightest. The reviewer's condescending tone, the balance he maintains between spurious flattery and presumptuous censure, which does not allow his victim to reveal that his remarks have struck home; scraps of sentences, scattered with careful calculation throughout the text, which now are embedded inside her head with a hundred little barbs. "A beautiful, tender, feminine nature" who had received "rather absurd commendation in a press notice"—as if she had any control over the views expressed in the press! Words like "straitlaced" and "fool's fool." But above all the line: Many people mistake for original ideas what are merely reminiscences.

The first frenzy of remorse that she has allowed others to see her wearing her heart on her sleeve has subsided. For Clemens, who appears indignant over the affair with the reviewer and very probably feels so as well, she puts on an air of equanimity. But she has been invaded by a subtle and inexpugnable poison, emanating from those lines in the review, and along with it by a new kind of dread. She feels an almost irresistible temptation to give up, let herself go. To go away, to creep away and hide, to search out that ultimate, undetectable hiding place where no one, neither friend nor foe, can ferret her out. She will not allow herself to be humiliated. She has the remedy to prevent this, and she will not hesitate to use it. What consolation lies in the knowledge that one does not have to live.

Clemens, in his excess of zeal, describes the counterfeit praise of this literary hack as petty, his censure as rather ill-bred, the writer himself as lacking in finesse, as a scribbler for a paper that is read by every shop boy.

Clemens, she says at last, that's enough. For me it is an established fact that I must write. There is a longing in me to express my life in enduring form. And no approbation of my poems has given me as much pleasure as yours has. But do you really believe I am so infatuated with myself that I do not know how far I am from turning this longing into reality?

Surely Clemens, whom she admires so, must know: dissatisfaction with oneself is the true thorn in one's flesh. This shame—he must have a more intimate acquaintance with it than she.

Bettine with her troubled glances. Of course it was she who appointed her brother to come along across the river here from Offenbach. Yet Günderrode felt a distinct pang when, upon her arrival, he was the first person she saw, and beside him the Mereau woman, Sophie—no doubt about it, she was a beauty—the former wife of the Jena professor, whom Clemens had courted with such unremitting zeal that in the end—confused and uncertain as to whom her heart really inclined—she followed the man who most ruthlessly laid siege to her.

Günderrode read the entire emotional saga of Sophie Mereau in the latter's first glance: conscience-stricken, defiant, exultant, and despairing. Her child? Yes, fortunately he was well now, out of danger.

How happy she was to hear it! Günderrode embraced Sophie, which seemed to astonish and delight her. Günderrode had often found that other women valued her opinion; why, she did not understand. Sophie, she said, a child! You must feel so proud. I know of nothing more important than having a child. She was almost tempted to add: I shall never have one myself.

Clemens, who was observing the encounter between the two women with something approaching anxiety, chose to intervene. How fit Sophie was; and he described how, just two weeks after a difficult delivery, she had climbed some . dangerous mountains with him. One could, he maintained, turn her upside down, and she would always land on her feet.

The two women came to an understanding: how childish men are.

Clemens, swelled with the pride of ownership, continued talking about his child. On the whole he was quite pleased with him and felt great delight when he held him.

A garrulous delight, dear Clemens, Sophie interjected.

Perhaps, he replied, slightly miffed. I don't dare to really love him with all that is in me. He is quite capable of simply packing up my love and traveling off with it into the other world.

There, now you've heard it for yourself, said Mereau to Günderrode. He has never yet dared really to love one single human being with all that is in him. What he really loves is telling other people about it.

Now he was really being wrongfully accused! Clemens cried in a plaintive tone, and his wife adopted the same bantering note; all three of them laughed. Bettine joined them, looked them over quizzically, and then said that they were singular people: their eyes spoke a different language from their mouths. Her brother called her a saucy sprite and pulled her hair. Later Günderrode quietly told Bettine that one day she intended to give some thought to the question of what it implied that the most serious and painful things between human beings were expressed in the guise of a masquerade, and of whether so many smiling mouths did not conceal some grave malady on the part of society as a whole.

Bettine understood her at once. She merely asked that Günderrode be lenient toward her brother, who in his heart of hearts was good, and also unhappy.

But I bear him no ill will whatsoever! Even Bettine does not believe it. I myself often find it strange that I am incapable of hatred, that I forget the offenses committed against me, but never forget a wrong I have done someone else. Why do they force me to call to mind again that calamitous hour?

On one point she has really raked her conscience over the coals and concluded: she gave him no pretext, much less any right, to seek to overwhelm her as he did. She knows that the members of Frankfurt society call her a coquette: a fact which, to be sure, reflects the usual jealousy of middle-class women who may happen to be undesired themselves; but it hurts her all the same. She knows too well the causes which can trigger in a woman some unconscious response to a man: mere self-absorption, the dread of an ignominious loneliness. The man, driven by egotism to think himself irresistible, has the knack of interpreting such signals, no matter how covert, as an open invitation. She must be on guard against herself, all the more so because she considers herself capable of an uncalculating and boundless self-surrender. But in Clemens's case she is quite certain that he misjudged her. She must tell him so.

He must marvel, he tells her, at her firm and pervasive conviction of her own worth, at the way she takes it upon herself, to an extent uncommon for one of her sex, to assume this air of self-righteousness. She is arrogant, is she aware of that?

This is not the first time that Günderrode has heard herself accused of arrogance. It is senseless to try to defend herself against the charge. I know my shortcomings, she says. They lie elsewhere than where you seek them.

This fact that we cannot ever count on being known for what we are.

This woman is inflexible, and hence she has no need to be imperious. In Kleist she awakens strange memories. Now, as she laughs in that conciliatory way, touching Brentano lightly on the shoulder as if she were begging his forgiveness, while on the mantelpiece the ornate little clock strikes a rarefied chord which no one hears but himself—just now he is remembering the loosened hairpins of his Wilhelmine. He sees himself and her, as it were, in the flesh, in the summerhouse behind the Zenge house in Frankfurt an der Oder, screened by the dense woodbine from the gazes of others, with the book Voss's *Luise* lying on the little white table between them. Wilhelmine, her head bowed, in a tender mood, permits him to unbind her hair, the feel of which his fingertips have not forgotten. He still knows, and always will, what he felt then: embarrassment and guilt. Now he is moved by this picture. Why then had it left him so cold, so excruciatingly cold, when it had not been a faraway dumb show but an actual hour of love between him, the lover who, God knows, was called upon to act, not to observe, and Wilhelmine, the poor girl—no fantasy image like that miniature of her, which, by the way, he had returned to her as propriety demanded—but his own tender fiancée, close beside him? The delicate aroma of disillusionment permeates the whole incident.

Oh, this innate bad habit of always existing in places where I do not live, or in a time which is past or is yet to come.

Then, just before the image fades at his mental command, he thinks of something which he does not wish to acknowledge: it was then, with Wilhelmine, that he had spoken, for the first and only time, about his dream. He has a need to communicate his innermost secrets, and thus —with what prodigious effort!—he has had to erect mighty ramparts inside himself against this need. He sometimes thinks that the speech impediment which afflicts him in social situations represents a remedy by which nature chooses to aid him by guaranteeing his silence. This notion is consonant with his present concept of nature. But that afternoon with Wilhelmine, oppressed by a lack of responsiveness in himself which he did not want to own up to and yet wished to explain, he broke his vow and told his betrothed about the dream which had afflicted him ever since he had left military service, and from which he invariably awoke in tears. He always saw a shaggy beast, it seemed to be a boar, a wild, beautiful, raging creature which he was pursuing at a breathless gallop in order to bridle it, mount it, and subdue it. He would be within one stride of catching up with it, its tawny pelt right before his eyes, his flesh grazed by its hot breath—but he could never succeed in reaching it. And each accursed time, when he was so exhausted that he dropped to the ground and the beast was threatening to escape, he would, once again, reach for the musket which his omnipresent, unknown enemy held out to him, point it, take aim, and fire. The animal rearing up, plunging downward, shuddering in the agony of death.

Afterwards, he recalls, they were silent for a long time,

until he saw that Wilhelmine was crying. He asked her no questions, stroked her hand, and finally felt what before he had deeply regretted not feeling: that he could love her. Kleist, she said at last, seemingly composed: Nothing can come of the two of us. We will never be man and wife. In a few minutes they had experienced everything they could experience together, and yet—heaven knows why!—the relationship nevertheless dragged on its torturous way for years.

The old, useless grief, which he dreads, is attempting to overpower him. Wedekind is right, he must learn to break all the threads which bind him to the past. When a man takes so long to become aware of his vocation, he must indeed pay a high price for it. Why, oh why, can't I get that into my head?

That dream. That it should go on pursuing him all these years. That it should scarcely have changed, and, irrational as it might be, should each time shake him to his foundations. This can only mean that he finds himself, over and over, confronting the same fearful conflict. He has the choice—assuming that it can justly be called a choice—either to systematically annihilate in himself that consuming dissatisfaction which is the best thing in him, or to give free rein to it and be destroyed by his temporal misery. To create time and space in accordance with the necessity of his own being, or simply to vegetate in a run-of-the-mill existence. Really a neat touch, that. The Powers which have him in their clutches do not demean him by esteeming him lightly. This is the only compensation he will know in his life. And he is determined to show himself worthy of it. No one other than himself will execute judgment upon him. The hand which was fated to commit the crime will carry out the sentence. A destiny after his own heart. With a voluptuous shudder he beholds the inner machinery of the soul. He who grows accustomed to such visions, to such glances into the depths, falls prey to no other addiction, has no need of any other intoxicant. Not even of love. And never again will he know a guilt-free hour. He who plays for such high stakes—himself, his whole being—should not count on having companions. Nor on the commonplace happiness of being free to be completely truthful with other people.

Kleist begins to perspire, and in seconds his body is drenched with sweat. He feels himself turning pale; the weakness in his legs is back again. —Sit down, for heaven's sake! —The Privy Councilor. He can be relied on at moments like this. As if by chance, he arranges his broad heavy frame in front of Kleist in such a way as to screen him from the others. He hands Kleist a handkerchief and proceeds to ignore the whole incident, as they have trained themselves to do. With a sense of relief Kleist perceives that the attack is passing, the uneasiness receding before it has had a chance to turn into anguish, into nightmarish constriction. The ladies, Privy Councilor, he says, the ladies here truly astound me.

Yes, the ladies! The Privy Councilor could not agree with him more.

Jestingly, with a trace of complacency, he praises the Rhenish air, which, he is sure, encourages a different type of growth from the sandy soil of Prussia. Although he,

Wedekind, would not wish to be accused of esteeming too lightly those virtues which one can learn among the Prussians as nowhere else on earth: austerity, devotion to duty, self-discipline. Kleist hears the voices of his father, his uncle. Ah, he says in a tone courteous to the point of absurdity, outside Prussia people have exaggerated notions about the Prussian virtues. After all, he says, we Prussians are only human like everyone else.

He must simply be sure not to laugh, for once he started he would never stop.

By the way, you know Savigny? says the unsuspecting Wedekind. Surely you must have noticed him?

Kleist understands.

Wedekind has taught him a technique of counteracting his obsessive notion that everyone is secretly concerned with his failings. Summoning all his wits and faculties, he is supposed to concentrate on one member of the social circle in which he happens to find himself at the moment. In this way, so the theory went, his attention will be diverted from himself and toward someone else, and that sense of oppression which as a rule has terminated in melancholy will retreat.

So, Savigny. An unfortunate choice. Impossible not to notice him; impossible not to recognize when one is confronted with one's own antitype. The man who is like a signpost for all to read: the hand of nature can in fact shower good fortune on her creatures. The potentiality for perfection is not a myth. Savigny, the man who creates his own fate. Wealthy, independent, sovereign. Early in life grown conscious of his worth, perhaps even of his limitations. Bound to nothing but to plans and goals which are capable of realization. Appointed professor of jurisprudence—and why not? Kleist forbids himself to feel prejudice toward a man headed for some high official post. His mood is taking a turn for the worse, that much he can tell. Is he sinking so low as to envy this Savigny the secure, the free and easy way he deals with other people? His way with women, who find him irresistible? The fact that even Bettine, that whirlwind of a girl, calmed down and became almost meek after Savigny had taken her hand and spoken to her in that forcible but amiable manner— despite the fact that Kleist would swear that the self-assured man feels nothing for her but indifference?

It tears him apart to know that to them he counts for nothing. He has not yet written that work with which he will one day deliver these people, and all the others, such blows that they will sink to their knees. No presentiment informs them of the true identity of this mute stranger in their drawing room—that is, of what he himself imagines to be his true identity. They may have heard rumors. This is quite conceivable in view of the way gossip thrives in the homes of the wealthier classes along the Rhine and the Main. Kleist intercepts glances which rouse him to bitterness.

At last. They are being invited to take tea.

A fresh-looking, young-as-spring girl brings in the tray and is greeted by Bettine a shade too rapturously. Günderrode notes a certain distaste on the face of the guest from Prussia. She knows Bettine. To him it must seem extravagant and high-flown, the way she takes the girl's hand, calls her by name—Marie—and proclaims to everyone that the songs she tries out on the clavichord were all taught to her by this girl, who, in addition to her knowledge of folk songs and fairy tales, is unrivaled in her knowledge of the botanical features of the region. She takes two teacups from the tray and brings them to Günderrode and Clemens, announcing to Clemens that she has some real gems for his folk-song collection. Melodies which fit their text as if the two were drawn together by a magnet. Her brother is unresponsive, she asks no questions, casts a searching glance at his face and Günderrode's, and withdraws to the big oval table, where almost everyone, including Kleist, is taking his seat. Sweet pastry is handed around in filigree china hampers. For a moment there is complete silence. Günderrode hears her heartbeat, and a senseless hope surges through her. Then Gunda Savigny says: An angel just walked through the room.

Clemens makes a wry face. The rather sentimental nature of this other sister is not to his taste. Günderrode cannot permit herself to feel the slightest hostile impulse toward Gunda, for she knows that her friendship with Savigny will endure only if she adheres strictly to the rules: that the covenant between them is a covenant of three, and that Gunda is the third. Günderrode has to smile at that. Regardless of the protestations of the two others, it is not Gunda who is the third member of the pact: it is she. Love represents a stronger bond than friendship. Who should know that better than she?

She hears someone ask what she was laughing at. Oh, Clemens! Out with it now, he says; he is beginning to get used to her secretly making sport of him. After all, she left him in the dark for so long regarding her talents as a poet, and did not show him a single one of her efforts; and to really put him to shame, she had put this little volume of hers on the market behind his back.

Why had she come along with the others. She ought to have known herself better. The reasons she had used to talk herself into coming—the empty place in the Merten coach, the urgent pleas of her friends Paule and Charlotte Servière, those twins whose names everyone always mentioned in a single breath as if they were one person—had been mere pretexts. Now she perceives the true reason why she came and also understands why she put up that strange and violent resistance: she had to see Savigny again. There is always passion involved when we do something we do not want to do.

Clemens cannot get over the fact that he failed to remark in her nature that perfection clearly manifested in her poems. He had to weep, he says, at the wonderful aptness of his own sentiments; for he believes that he can trace reflections of them in her work.

Keep calm now. I see that I am still far from having trained myself to be prepared for anything.

Clemens, Günderrode replies, you would not have said that to a man. Why do you refuse to admit that in poetry, as if in a mirror, I attempt to collect and to see myself, to pass through and beyond myself. We have no control over how other people—posterity, let us say—will judge our worth, and I am not concerned about the matter. But everything we express must be the truth because we feel it: there you have my confession of faith as a poet.

All well and good, she says to herself; only don't get too high-flown, too bombastic and solemn and self-righteous. I may easily fail at both, both living and writing; but I have no choice. And even friendship denies me its happy deceptions.

Yes! says Clemens in a tone of unexpected bitterness, as if he had heard what she was thinking, that's the way you are. Always reserved, always perfectly under control. Always hard on yourself and others. Always suspicious. You don't love me, Karoline, and you never have.

Had they not agreed to keep silent on this score? She has had enough, more than enough, she is very tired. Now what is he saying? He is calling himself my best, my only true friend. If only he knew that now I am incapable of feeling anything but the dread of dying inside, nothing but horror of the wasteland which will grow and spread within me when I have lost my youth. My friend, my friends! I understand their glances only too well, I am not at home among them. There where my home is, love exists only at the price of death. And I marvel at the fact that, apart from me, no one appears to recognize this palpable truth, and that I am forced to conceal it within the lines of my poems like stolen goods. If only someone had the courage to take it literally, to express it in a natural voice like any other kind of public announcement. Then they would all learn the meaning of fear.

Suddenly she perceives—an experience which often befalls her—quite detached from herself and all the others, the pattern which would be formed by the configurations of the people in this room, in the shape of a graph, a diagram drawn on a gigantic sheet of white paper; a singular maze of lines of varying thickness, intersecting at many points or suddenly breaking off. An extraordinarily beautiful representation which hardly bears any relation to herself. She perceives the point which all the lines avoid, around which there has formed a patch of empty space: Kleist. Who knows no one but his doctor and who addresses no one but him. It touches her to see the way he jams his feet behind the chair legs, the way he goes on holding the teacup, which was empty long ago. Does courtesy demand that he be drawn into the conversation? Or does it rather decree that he be left in peace, something which he appears to value? Günderrode does not know how to interpret his gaze, which she has already intercepted several times.

Another of those who take themselves too seriously.

Kleist is thinking: Brentano seems to have claims on her. As Wedekind does on me.

There is no doubt of the fact that he owes the man his gratitude. Wedekind took him in as one ought to receive a man sick unto death—without reservations and without asking questions. Quite possibly, Wedekind saved his life. But where is it written that a man who has been saved from death must follow his savior wherever he wants to take him?

Kleist knows of no more tormenting emotion than shame.

As if he did not know what chains him to Wedekind. True, a doctor may be obligated to help someone who is sick; but Kleist can forgive neither himself nor Wedekind for the method used to preserve his life. It might be the height of ingratitude secretly to reproach the physician for having succeeded in relaxing the numbness, the stark staring rigidity of his patient, by employing against it the only remedy at his disposal: by getting him to talk. By gradually drawing out, with sympathetic questions, this man who considered himself completely destroyed and who obstinately refused to say a word. Kleist will never forget how good it felt, and at the same time how degrading, to finally give in and reply to Wedekind's cautious initiatives; how desperately he longed to do so, and at the same time abhorred the whole thing. For he had not failed to notice how the Privy Councilor was knotting together those sentences in which Kleist himself described his condition with a grisly precision, and forging them into a rope with which, bit by bit, he was pulling him out of danger. An image meant to be taken literally. When, returning from France, Kleist had broken down in Mainz, he felt that he was lying smashed to bits at the bottom of a deep shaft, and he could not stand anyone who did not share this feeling—including the doctor, in whose face were clearly inscribed the traits of health and emotional tranquillity. Reason, moderation, the husbanding of his energies—yes and again yes! How is the healthy man to understand the sick one? The Privy Councilor suppressed his admonitions in order to avoid irritating his patient. Kleist calmed down somewhat—a singular man—once he had found the simile which most clearly circumscribed his condition: he had fallen into the grinding mechanism of a mill, which was breaking each of his bones one by one, and at the same time tearing him to shreds.

No doubt about it: the man was suffering. The physician saw him writhing in pain, heard him groan as if he were on the rack. Kleist recalls that the pain extorted confessions from him, efforts to describe it. No one can stand it for long, Doctor. One day it must either let up or kill me.

Since that time Kleist has known that words are incapable of depicting the soul, and he believes that he will never be permitted to write again.

Then again he was walking through the cold wintry streets of Mainz in a state of unspeakable destitution which he mistook for peace, until a casual glance at a carved stone eagle above a gateway tore him up at the roots and drove him back to Wedekind's house in tears. Can you picture a man, Doctor, without any skin, who must walk around among people; who is tortured by every sound, blinded by every gleam of light, pained by the touch of the air, not matter how gentle? That's the way it is with me, Doctor. I'm not exaggerating. You must believe me.

I believe you, Wedekind said, not unmoved, and remained sitting by the bedside of the exhausted man, who, as if he were trying to hold on to himself, was squeezing his body with both arms and beating his head back and forth on the pillow, until at last he fell asleep. Not until very recently did the Privy Councilor indicate to his guest that he believed he had found the correct designation for his illness in the medical literature, along with an exact description. However, he said, he did not wish to call into question the intensity and dignity of Kleist's affliction by applying to it a dry scientific term. Moreover, he doubted whether science, whose method consisted in objective generalization, was applicable to cases of extreme personal distress, simply because it does not have access to that life-transforming empirical knowledge possessed by the afflicted person: the knowledge that there is in fact a pain so terrible that one can die of it.

The kind Privy Councilor. He must long have known that people prefer to break down beneath burdens which are self-imposed. But he has never before met a man like myself, Kleist reflects with perverse humor, who devotes such infernal precision to the task of contriving his own destruction. He has abandoned his dogma, by which he set such store, that man possesses free will, and his child-like faith that every affliction carries within it the seeds of its own cure was confounded by my case. Something is grinding you down, Kleist, of which you are not master. How true. The calamity, Privy Councilor, of being dependent on ties which suffocate me if I put up with them, and which tear me apart if I break free. This is a malady that does not grow attenuated with the years but merely cuts deeper and deeper.

The Privy Councilor, who has learned to fear this man's pride, may hope that Kleist has forgotten the degrading scenes that took place during their first few days together; but to Kleist's sorrow, he has not forgotten a thing. The fact that he wept, indeed shrieked, and that he implored the Privy Councilor, a total stranger, to take pity on him; that he allowed himself to be carried away to the point of betraying those names which branded him most deeply: Ulrike, Wilhelmine. The fact that he presented the image of a desperate man completely crushed by some guilt, by some failure, until one day Wedekind, beside himself, shook him by the shoulders and yelled at him: My God, man, what do you have to reproach yourself for! Whereupon Kleist ranted and raved until he was exhausted, then slept straight through a night and a day and, when he woke up, calmly and quietly declared that now he knew what he had to do: he was going to become a carpenter.

Kleist gnashes his teeth. If there were only some way to turn off the mechanism inside his head, which they had installed there instead of a normal memory, and which, no matter what he does, no matter where he goes or stays, and even during the night, when he starts bolt awake around 4:00 a.m., is incapable of doing anything but repeating the same train of thought over and over, the same everlasting tormenting monologue which he is forced to conduct on every single one of these innumerable days in order to defend himself against invisible accusers.

It's enough to drive one mad.

What was that you said?

I? Oh, nothing. Just a slip. A stupid habit.

Joseph Merten, their host. Wholesale dealer in foodstuffs and perfume in Frankfurt am Main. Amateur of the arts and sciences.

I do hope you're feeling quite up to snuff! Very well indeed. Couldn't be better. Very much obliged. Surely the man is not one of those clods who feel compelled to decorate their middle-class salons with one or two peers of the realm, no matter how paltry and down-at-heel they may be. To be sure, Wedekind did assure him that the propinquity of the Rhineland to France had at least achieved something, having rendered completely unfashionable pretentious customs of this kind. That I can well believe! Kleist had cried. That's the only thing this degenerate people is still capable of: doing away with a couple of obsolete fashions.

Kleist! Is it really possible that you hate the French!

Indeed, I do hate them. He thinks: As one hates what one has loved too dearly.

In many respects this man remains a riddle to the physician. Once he began to recuperate, he again withdrew completely into himself. When he speaks, he gives one the impression that he is doing so quite voluntarily rather than in response to a compulsion. All confidences have ceased. If one succeeds in irritating him into gathering his energies enough to utter some sarcastic remark, one has won what there is to win.

One day, maintaining the same jocular tone throughout, Kleist expounded to the Privy Councilor's family a discourse on the subject of how difficult it is to burn papers, especially when one has nothing to burn them in but a miserable, plugged-up, malodorous, smoking old dragon of a stove. But when the flames finally do begin to lick the edges of the leaves and the pages writhe in the heat, flare up, and turn black, what a feeling of exultation and relief seizes hold of you. How free you feel. How incredibly free.

Free? Of what?

Kleist gave a forced laugh. Free of obligations which one may merely have talked oneself into believing must be fulfilled.

That was all they could get out of him on the subject. If only the Privy Councilor has not read that letter, the letter from Wieland, which he had intended to be torn to shreds by an English bullet along with his heart. "You must complete your *Guiscard* even if the entire Caucasus or the entire globe were weighing you down." Good heavens, how embarrassing. Wedekind must believe that this was the tone customary among devotees of the literary arts, and by this view it would be only logical to conclude that a man with a severely overstrained nervous system had been the victim of the inordinate demands of his friends.

Who am I. A lieutenant without a sword knot. A student without learning. A civil servant without a post. An author without a book.

Melancholia. The best course would be to get so used to using this formula that it becomes second nature to him: obviously it is going to come in handy.

Only never to write again. Everything else, but not that.

Günderrode is cutting across the room at an angle and coming toward him to fetch his empty cup. That one should be unable to leave a party when one wants to simply because one is dependent on someone else's coach. How slowly the minutes creep by. What's going on? It appears that Bettine wants to remove something from Günderrode's little drawstring bag. Clumsy thing. She drops it, something shiny slips out and slides across the smooth parquet floor. Very strange: a dagger. The alert Kleist picks up the weapon, hands it to Günderrode.

A curious device to be found in a young lady's toiletries bag, Fräulein.

Curious? Perhaps. To me it seems quite natural.

Bettine wrests the dagger away from her. For a long time, she says, she has wanted to get a closer look at it. Who would have dreamed that Günderrode actually carried it on her person!

Everyone has stood up as if in response to some signal. Without intending to, Kleist hears Savigny ask her softly: All the time? And Günderrode's reply: All the time. Savigny shakes his head with a troubled look. The dagger is passed from hand to hand, everyone tests the blade, adjudges it sharp, admires the silver pommel. Everyone knows about Günderrode's dagger; Kleist can only marvel at it all. Charlotte and Paule Servière, those enchanting twins, engage in a mock duel. Wedekind intervenes, confiscates the weapon, and declares, half in earnest, that as a physician he has the right to hold on to it because it is a demonstrable threat to life and limb.

That you will *not* do, says Günderrode with an uncommon gravity, and amid universal silence the Privy Councilor gives the dagger back to her with a courteous bow. Serenely she stows it away in her bag.

An impenetrable incident. Just the right moment for the folding door to open and a servant to bring in some wine. But the invitation had spoken only of tea! Merten will not listen to any objections. After all, he says, they were in wine country, so one could hardly think of his wine as a special treat. Besides, this wine is from his own vineyard and he will vouch for its quality. One can see that the man enjoys drinking.

Kleist has observed that Savigny has been put out of humor by the game with the dagger. Moreover, he also has the impression that Günderrode wishes to take Savigny aside and speak with him alone; but the latter takes no notice of her gesture and seizes on Kleist as a welcome excuse for turning away: I hear that you've recently been in Paris?

Brilliant, Savigny. One must grant you that, my friend: you're a past master at keeping people dangling.

The light grows dim and I am standing in the darkness, alone.

Günderrode hates being dependent on so many things to which she does not wish to concede any influence over her life; and more than anything else she hates to be caught in the act of being dependent. The shame. Günder-rode-my-pet is very kind but quite weak, people had said· to Savigny, and he had told her about it. Now he is giving Kleist a long-winded account of his plan to go to Paris in pursuit of his studies. Kleist appears to be maintaining his reserve. Paris? Well, of course, for a genuine scholar ... Ah, Savigny again: Surely Kleist, as a literary man, does not feel he failed to get his money's worth out of his Parisian sojourn?

Empty chatter. What if all the mouths in the world suddenly went dumb and thoughts became audible. One of those licentious desires for which Savigny would reprove her. In a sense, it is a kind of pose with you, he might well say ... The famous chiaroscuro, Günderrode my pet, keeping a balance between light and dark. I mean that you would by no means be living up to your true nature if you never showed most people any other side of you than this.

How well I know him. Do not be too tender and too melancholy and too yearning—be lucid and stable and yet full of *joie de vivre*. Ah, Savigny. What does all that really mean? It means that Günderrode-my-pet is not supposed to molest you further. She is not only supposed to understand what is appointed to her: to stand in the background and wait, to play second fiddle, but she is also supposed to keep quiet about it. And—this of course was the most agreeable, the most convenient thing of all—she was supposed to be cheerful about it, that horrid little Günderrode-my-pet, your dear little duck. She is not supposed to make anyone feel the least twinge of guilty conscience. —And of course he is right.

He is also in the right in relation to Kleist. I can tell that by his face, which remains detached and superior while Kleist is being foolish enough to get himself worked up. But look, he is stuttering, or whatever you call it. He has a speech impediment which interrupts the flow of his sentences, makes him falter—perhaps only when he gets excited as he is just now. What, can they really be saying what I think they are? Are they quarreling about Rousseau? Rousseau, the Prussian cries, is the fourth watchword in a Frenchman's mouth, right after *liberté, égalité, fraternité*. Yet how ashamed Rousseau would be if he were to come to Paris now and were told that the state of things there was his handiwork.

She had to warn the young man. Savigny is more than a match for anyone once he gets on this tack. She can predict the tone in which he will reply to Kleist: a tone of boundless amazement. What! he asks—yes, in precisely that tone—You would look to find the traces of Rousseau's ideas in contemporary France! To this Kleist, cooled down now and affecting an unapproachability bordering on the comic, in turn replies: Indeed, yes. Why else are ideas brought into the world, if not to be fulfilled in reality?

Günderrode can see the thoughts inside Savigny's well-constructed head. Oh, so he's one of those. One of the fanatical kind. She knows with what little success she herself has often attempted to defend herself against his censure, and even more against his clemency; how deeply she has been seared by the desire to see him suffer; how she suffered when she confessed to herself that she no longer had any control over the depth of sympathy he elicited from her, and when the growing intensity of her emotions taught her that what she felt was not sympathy but passion. And when her vulnerability and her upbringing and all the circumstances of her life bade her conceal from him what she felt. Her attempt succeeded, perhaps too well, for she is mistress of the art of dissimulation. Once he actually reproached her for this—indirectly, to be sure, for they never spoke of this most important of matters except by indirection. People talk a lot about the sorrows of young Werther, he had said, but other people had also had their sorrows, and simply never described them in print. She has read this sentence of his a hundred, a thousand times, without ever wearing it out, and from it she draws some palliation for all the humiliations which, in part because of this same sentence, she has inflicted on herself. Your letter made me so happy, so truly happy, deep down . . .

Is it still true? Has everything really changed? Can such a thing be? And it doesn't hurt any more, Savigny, or not very much, when one dispenses with the need for self-deception? I wanted to tell you how monstrously unnatural it would be if we two failed to become close, close friends . . .

Your hand, Savigny: does it still hurt?

What? I beg you, Karoline! Here I am trying to get this young poet to acknowledge the boundary between philosophy and life . . .

Your hand, Savigny. It doesn't hurt any more now, does it?

No, Günderrode my pet, since you insist on knowing. You see? It was only that blow you received from the coach door. You did not honestly get burned.

Physicians make mistakes, everyone knows that. But that Someone who closed the coach door on my hand hurt me terribly, that you must believe.

Very likely I must. The tale of your ailing hand is very pretty indeed. I feel that this way I am fonder of your hand than I would have been if it had always been well and whole.

Just do not forget, Günderrode my pet, that you are no longer merely my friend, but *our* friend as well.

How could I forget, Savigny. The two of you, Gunda and you, now form a part of my fate.

It is thus that we speak when we are dreaming, or when we have leave to utter our final words on this earth. Kleist is in no way interfering with this dream conversation. He feels this clearly and experiences no urge to withdraw.

If only I were your brother, Savigny. Or Gunda's sister.

Günderrode-my-pet, you are a silly little Günderrode-my-pet.

And so it went on and on, as if they were sleepwalkers without any fear of falling down a precipice. Given the fact that it outrages my feelings to be dependent on anything in the world, and not to be completely unfettered and, quite simply, the most important person in the world to anyone with whom I have a relationship—just think, what I often want is to break free of you both by dint of courage and strength, and to lead a separate, happy life of my own.

What strange feelings and resolutions, Günderrode. You have downright republican attitudes. A little hangover from the French Revolution, do you suppose? Well, in that case you would surely find yourself in agreement with our friend here, who steadfastly refuses to take my word for it that it is a beneficent arrangement to keep the realm of thoughts neatly cordoned off from the realm of action.

No doubt he will ask you wherein this supposed benefaction consists.

That is in fact exactly what he did just ask me. And I say to him and to you: The benefaction lies in the freedom of thought we owe to this sage arrangement. Or do the two of you really refuse to see what restrictions would be imposed on all thought if we had to be afraid that our fantasies might conceivably find a gate by which to enter into reality. In the name of heaven, no: it is the law that we are not supposed to take philosophy literally or measure real life by the ideal.

The question remains: Is this law always valid? Valid without exception?

Indeed it is. It is the law of laws, Kleist, on which rest all our human institutions with their inevitable flaws, their tendency to crack. He who rebels against it must become a criminal. Or a madman.

Ha, Kleist cries, as if in delight. But I really must thank you most kindly for saying that. You are teaching me to understand Goethe.

You'll have to explain that to me.

Later, Savigny, perhaps later. So philosophy—you say it yourself—has become groundless, without foundation. You can take this quite literally. And if you had been in France as I was and had seen what I was forced to see, you would know what I am talking about. All the proofs of philosophy have undergone a permutation, and the ground has been pulled out from underneath our thoughts.

"Tendency to crack"—*his* words coming out of Savigny's mouth. Kleist falls silent. Now he is standing alone at the window, and one would swear that he does not see the landscape which he appears to be looking at and which, if he did in fact perceive it, might well elicit from him an exclamation of joy or recognition. They claim that it is possible for a man to spend his whole life with the land of his birth right there in front of his eyes, and notice nothing but pine woods, level green lakes, fields of rye, turnips, and potatoes. Kleist believes that he can hear the whispering of their thoughts behind his back. The clock strikes four. How slowly time is passing, and in the room behind him the people are moving about unperturbed, in that spontaneous, irreproachable style which they appear to regard as a valid form of life. The manners which are tolerated—or perhaps expected—here are new to him and not without a certain allure. All of them, he thinks, all of them, with only a few exceptions, misjudge me, fail to appreciate my worth.

You are quite right, a voice says beside him. There are words which one does not expect to hear from Savigny.

The tendency to crack, says Kleist. But how did you know . . .

The corners of her mouth were twitching.

People ought to be on their guard against you.

Most of them are.

Ought we not to do as most people do? What other choice is there? Is there another way of talking besides theirs?

I was just thinking, says Kleist, almost believing that

he had in fact been thinking this—about what would be the opposite of the tendency to crack.

Consensus, says Günderrode. Convention.

I see you know the world. But am I correct in thinking that I hear no contempt in your voice?

Ought we to feel contempt for something so powerful and so necessary as convention?

Something, therefore, to which one must by rights adhere.

If one can. Absolutely.

A Delphic oracle. Kleist does not like that. The only people who have the right to speak of the tendency to crack are those who have some personal experience of it. This woman, who appears to be endowed with a sixth sense regarding the emotions of others, drops the subject and asks, although now in the most conventional tone in the world: I hear that you have been in this area before?

Kleist does his duty. Twice. The last time with my sister. I know the riverbank along here, at least from on board a boat.

The trip along the Rhine with Ulrike, which, like any prolonged period he has spent alone with her, ended in discord and misunderstanding. We both know why, but we dare not confess it. I was deeply affected by the landscape. These Günderrodes and Brentanos would be amazed at the reactions of the unimpressionable Prussian if they could hear what he had written in letters to his friends, and what today he could still repeat from memory without the slightest deviation: But the most beautiful stretch of land in Germany, on which our great Gardener obviously labored *con amore*, is that along the banks of the Rhine from Mainz to Koblenz, which we sailed past along the river itself. The whole region is a sort of poet's dream, and the most luxuriant imagination could conceive of nothing lovelier than this valley, which now opens, now closes, now is full of blooming vegetation and now is a desert, now laughs and now fills one with dread.

Reading this, even Brentano, who was born under a lucky star and who became famous overnight and with far too great an ease, would surely sit up and take notice, embrace the stranger, and prophesy to the gathering that one day, if there were any justice in the world, sentences like these would be found in every German student anthology. And all too easily, and over and over, we allow ourselves to be tempted, as we are led past the evidence of our own graves, into thinking that one day there will in fact be justice in the world and we will be judged on the basis of our inherent dignity and worth, and not in terms of our propriety, names, and social status. The rankest fantasy.

Just now, a rare thing to behold, the three Brentanos are standing together in the middle of the room. Clemens, Gunda, and Bettine smile at each other as only brothers and sisters smile, raise their glasses in a toast, clink them together, drink. There is a startling family resemblance, less in their features than in gestures, attitudes. This, Kleist believes, is the way people move when they regard themselves as indispensable in this world. He assumes the prerogative of pronouncing them presumptuous because inevitably they remain ignorant of this lack of self-doubt which is their heritage. In any case, they are all alluring, including the man, each in his or her own way. The dark eyes, the pale forehead, the crisp dark brown hair. A strain of Italian blood there, Wedekind had intimated. And the fluency of those puffed up in their own conceit. No impediments in *their* speech, no stammering tongues. Despite their high-strung, extravagant natures—he must grant them that—there is that in their physical build, their appearance, their mannerisms which one is accustomed to call noble. Real thoroughbreds.

Enough, enough. Always this thirst for fame and glory, this nonsense which his brain manufactures of its own accord whenever he is weak enough not to keep it under close guard. Student anthologies! He is making himself ridiculous.

He dimly remembers having once complained to the doctor about how much it torments him that the music inside him has turned mute. Except of course for those nerve-shattering discordant notes which last autumn, in his hideously empty room in Paris which never ceased to smell of cold smoke, gave him this headache which then mounted to such a pitch of intensity that merely in order to be free of it he would willingly have consented to having the whole world shift its axis.

There, he's done it again. Nothing disgusts him so much as these literary turns of phrase which are never geared to the height of our suffering—for then we are mute like any animal—but which rather set in afterwards, and are never free of deceit and vanity. "Would willingly have consented!" As if, when his anguish had driven him from the hated city of Paris and through the mist-shrouded plain of northern France toward the coast, he had not in actual fact quite wittingly reversed the poles of his life. When, namely, he decided to place himself under the command of that devil in human form, the archfiend Napoleon, in order to meet death in his service on the isle of Britain, instead of fleeing him to the ends of the earth.

This serpent's coil inside his head. Kleist is beginning to forget the reasons for his eccentric journey. The insight into his actions which he must have possessed at the time is slipping away from him. Now he feels compelled to insist, in the teeth of all opposition, that he has been barred any access to that period of his past. Melancholic— Wedekind's catchword, imprecise and enigmatic enough to screen all that business from the view of others, and even from himself. For in the long run no human being can live with the knowledge that, strongly as he may resist the world's evil, the drive within him to surrender unconditionally to this same evil is just as strong. And that the name he confers on the evil is merely a sort of substitute inspired by his dread of other designations. Napoleon. Kleist perceives how the grisly word swells up and sucks its fill of all his hatred, resentment, and self-contempt. And he also perceives—although surely this cannot be true—how all the turbid rivers of his soul are attracted by this same name and greedily flow toward it, as to the place which has been apportioned to them.

Never has he been able to tell any human being—nor does he know it himself or even wish to know it—how, when the accursed Corsican refused to perform that one little favor for a man desirous of death, abandoned his own plans, failed to send his fleet to England, and omitted to prepare for the desperate Kleist the battlefield he had longed for, Kleist had left that French coast made desolate by November, and returned to Paris, whence, under strict marching orders from the Prussian ambassador, he had set out for Potsdam and arrived as far as Mainz.

A broken instrument, mended only on the surface, which will no longer produce a sound. Something which is not worth smashing or bothering to spare. A propitious state of affairs, Doctor, without hope, without obligation. The most propitious of states.

Kleist?

Just once in my life, Privy Councilor, I should like to meet someone who, without subjecting me to any secret reproach, would simply permit me to be the person I am.

How can a person get along in the world if he is incapable of accommodating himself to the existing order.

Nature has given many people immunity to any form of intemperance. They automatically repel all inordinate acts and thoughts. Kleist recalls, not without a certain satisfaction, the moment when the doctor recoiled from him as if from the Devil himself. This man, whose finest quality is his professional curiosity, asked Kleist what a man feels when he burns papers which are infinitely precious to him. Without a moment's hesitation, and with an expression on his face which the doctor later felt compelled to call fanatical, Kleist replied: I saw Nothingness lying wide open before me.

Then the Privy Councilor broke off the conversation.

He gave up trying to understand his patient. This suited Kleist perfectly. He began to travel to Wiesbaden more frequently and spent both day and night at the parsonage, putting up with the sly looks which Wedekind afterwards cast his way, and with the doctor's comments on the incomparable curative powers of the feminine nature. He saw: Marianne, the pastor's daughter, a naïve child, did not even dare to think of what others already accepted as proven fact. Kleist used to go walking with her in the environs of the town and told her about his travels. He responded to the troubled glance of the pastor, a prudent man, with a shake of the head. It did him good that he could come and go as he pleased and that no one had any claims upon him. But a trifling change in the girl's behavior, traces of constraint, served as a signal to warn him that he could no longer spend time with her without awakening certain expectations. The same old story. I'm leaving this place, Privy Councilor. Soon.

To be sure, Kleist, no doubt that is the right thing to do. But come now, that's no reason to feel sad.

Kleist says that he wants to tell him a parable which—he must not take it amiss—has to do with the Privy Councilor's dog. That is, if he does not consider it unseemly to absent himself from the rest of the party for so long.

The sheerest mockery. No one cares in the least what they do. Those members of the gathering who have known each other for a long time are eager to continue their conversations, exactly identical to the ones they have always had, and take only a passing interest in the affairs of a stranger. At last Günderrode has collared Savigny.

She feels that this afternoon something of decisive importance still remains to be said. She feels this despite the fact that she knows perfectly well that all the real decisions were made long ago. They have left a residue that is poisoning her. Does she feel a need for some kind of reparation? Is she making one last attempt to obtain from someone else an absolute understanding of her nature? She decides to adopt a mocking pose.

To win your favor, Savigny, it is not enough merely to be outstanding in every way. For, if it were, you would necessarily have to be dreadfully in love with me, which I do not believe to be the case. Humbly I lay all my perfections at your feet; but you trample all over them as if they were cobblestones. Tell me now, how can one earn your love?

Have I not warned you, Günderrode my pet, never again, in my presence, to wear a certain gold watch on a chain around your neck? And what do I see but that you are wearing it anyhow.

Because I know, Savigny, that no little gold watch, and indeed nothing whatever on or about Günderrode, can possibly represent any threat to you. But do tell me whether the magic cipher which I sewed into your flannel after your wedding day is proving efficacious or not.

You wish to know how a person can go about earning my love. But you have known for a long time what quality is necessary, in addition to general excellence: the proper balance between independence and self-surrender.

I had thought to hear something a little more original from you, Savigny.

You are not listening carefully, Günderrode my pet; I can tell by the tone of your voice. I have often complained to you of your lack of trust, your exaggerated inclination to autonomy.

You are very kind. You say "exaggerated" in order to avoid saying "presumptuous." The fact that you forbade me to address you in the familiar—*du*—was also significant, highly significant. After all, one final touch was still lacking. That prohibition made things complete. But I am not complaining. He who misjudges another must bear the lion's share of the blame.

Undisciplined, unpredictable, inordinate, extreme. Oh, Savigny. After all, it was only a poem, even if, admittedly, it was too rash, too ungoverned a gesture. "The Kiss in the Dream." What could that mean to you just two weeks before your wedding? "A kiss breathed into me the breath of life . . ." And I was compelled to add that I no longer knew myself: that's true. This is the kind of thing little Günderrode-my-pet dreams about, and of whom does she dream? Of someone who is very dear and whom she will always love.

Oh, Savigny. A person cannot do any more than feel ashamed. You could have kept quiet about it and let it pass. You could have maintained silence in the presence of a pain which, as you must clearly feel, is completely genuine. Just as you must have felt that I was well and truly enslaved. —I just thought "was."

Savigny! I just thought "was."

And so? What delights you so about that? May one know?

No, Savigny. One may not know. There is in fact no need that one know everything. The essential thing is that one of us knows. But that brings to mind a little story which I simply must tell you. A few years ago I was standing with a certain young man on the balcony in the garden of the Leonhardi estate. We were alone, and I would very much have liked to talk with him, but a certain feeling of constriction, or perhaps even the pounding of my heart, held me back. This young man was also silent for a time, until at last he appeared to decide that it was improper that we should remain silent for so long. He asked me: How are things with your brother? Is he still in Hanau? This question made an extremely unpleasant impression on me. It gave me a feeling that I really cannot bear. Tell me your opinion, could not the young man have found something far more appropriate to ask me?

Quite so, dear friend. Savigny deserved that. Pay back that stupid Savigny for his stupidity.

The way you have of always seeing only yourselves. How spiteful, how ironic, how abominable your friend is being once again, is that what you're thinking?—instead of being tender and merciful. But all I wanted to say about it was this: Now I know why we were compelled to dash past each other like two blind young dogs, and I should like you to know the reason, too.

Haven't you always been rather given to straying, dear friend, even in your friendship?

And doesn't this question show, dear Savigny, that all this time you have in fact known nothing about your friend, your sister, your Günderrode-my-pet? That my nature made you uneasy because it sets you riddles? That you did not wish to take the trouble to find out which to believe: your personal observations, or that Rumor which represented me now as flirtatious, another time as prudish, now as a forceful and masculine spirit, and another time as the epitome of pliant femininity? That Rumor which is incapable of doing what a friend ought to do; namely, to see the true face behind all the façades?

Go ahead and scold away, Günderrode my pet. Savigny deserves it.

I'm quite serious, dear friend. My heart has turned away from you. It has just occurred to me that this is what I have been trying to tell you all this time, and you can see for yourself that I don't shrink from saying it. I lead a very active life, Savigny. I'm having Müller's history of Switzerland read aloud to me, I'm applying myself with great diligence to the study of Schelling, and—I feel like a fool to tell you—I am writing a drama, and my whole being is wrapped up in it. I project myself so vividly into the drama, I become so much at home within it, that my own life is becoming alien to me. Do you understand, Savigny, I know of no better life for me than this. Gunda says that it's foolish to let oneself be dominated to this degree by such minor artistry as mine. But I love this flaw in me, if indeed it is a flaw. Often it makes up to me for everything else. And it helps me to believe in the necessity of all things, even that of my own nature, imperfect as it may be. Without it, dear Savigny—this much I must tell you—I would not even be alive. And now let us never speak on the matter again.

What a long peroration, dear friend. Savigny will not forget it.

Out of the corners of his eyes Kleist sees the two of them getting up. He believes that he perceives in Savigny's face an unexpected emotion, in Günderrode's expression an unexpected fixity of purpose. Savigny bows over her hand, holding the pose for a long time. Then they separate swiftly, she going over to Bettine, who has been waiting for her in the window alcove, while he joins the group of men which, for reasons of courtesy or of personal interest, is forming around Kleist.

It is four-thirty.

Wedekind, undoubtedly happy to be relieved of the strain of being alone with his charge, regales the company —after first asking Kleist's permission—with an anecdote concerning an incident which Kleist claims to have witnessed, involving Wedekind's dog. Bello, an inoffensive and faithful animal who befriended Kleist during the first few days that their guest was in his master's house, later used to accompany him on his far-ranging walks. One day, Wedekind continued, Kleist had seen the dog, who had always delighted in obeying orders, trapped between two contradictory commands, each of which necessarily appeared to him absolutely binding. First, Wedekind's wife had called to him from the kitchen window, ordering him, as she so often did, to guard the Privy Councilor's youngest baby daughter. Second, Kleist whistled to him from the street, signaling his desire that the dog come walking with him. Then the dog, in a ghastly state of indecision, began to run back and forth between the kitchen window and the courtyard gate, and—so Kleist had assured Wedekind—the beast wore an expression of distress on his face. In order to discover the results of the experiment, neither Kleist nor the Privy Councilor's wife had released the animal from one of the commands. The dog had obviously been overwhelmed by the conflict. His eyes had glazed over with that thin film whose appearance signals that a dog is tired, and overcome by an irresistible urge to sleep, he had lain down exactly halfway between Kleist and Frau Wedekind and had fallen asleep on the spot.

Everyone marvels, laughs, applauds. Kleist, now the center of attention, adds: Yes, Frau Wedekind and I also had a good laugh at the animal's curious behavior. It was not until later, when I had thought about it a little, that I said to myself: The poor dog. And while the gentlemen discuss the incident, he is thinking: If only one could sleep one's whole life away.

Unfortunately, Wedekind feels compelled to make an inopportune remark. Herr von Kleist, he says smiling, appears to feel that to a certain extent he is in the same situation as the good dog Bello.

In what sense, everyone asks. Kleist fervently wishes that he had not said anything about the matter. One is always punished for every self-exposure. As curtly as possible he says: Well, the comparison between the animal and himself was merely a jest, even though it was impossible to overlook the similarity between the dog's situation and certain insoluble dilemmas in the lives of human beings.

For example? This is Merten, their host. It flatters him that such profound conversations are being held in his house.

He who asks a question must have an answer. For example, says Kleist, consider the following case: whether rightly or wrongly, someone feels in himself the compulsion to follow a certain vocation. His circumstances do not permit him to live abroad, where he would be free to pursue his plans, nor do they permit him to go on living in his native land without taking a civil-service post. But this post, which he would be forced to degrade himself beyond endurance to obtain, would in every way run counter to his vocation. *Voilà*. There you have your example.

Everyone is silent. At last Merten, who openly confesses to having read Kleist's drama *The House of Schroffenstein* and who would never believe that he is inflicting great torment on its author by his question, asks whether Herr von Kleist might not perhaps be able to earn a modest income from the sale of his literary productions?

Write books for money? Never! cries Kleist with unexpected vehemence. Shall I have resisted aims alien to my own in a sphere of activity to which I am indifferent and bear no affinity—the military—only to submit to these aims in that sphere which is most my own?

For heaven's sake, to whom am I saying all this? Kleist experiences one of those moments of doleful lucidity when he perceives the thought behind every play of features, the meaning behind every word, the reason for every action—moments when everything, most of all he himself, lies exposed in its nakedness and poverty, and loathing enters into him, and words are like toads jumping out of his mouth and the mouths of others. He feels strangely moved by the comment which wafts in his direction from Günderrode, who has sat down beside Bettine on a window seat: Poems are a balm laid upon everything in life that is unappeasable. Remarkable the way, even when this woman is speaking to other people, what she says appears to be intended for him, and that she seems to him the only person who is truly real in a horde of specters.

Then Brentano says in a grave tone which disposes Kleist in his favor: You're right, Kleist. In our times it's impossible to write poetry. One can only try to do something for poetry. The poet lives, as it were, in a wilderness, prey to the attack of wild beasts, for not all of them can be tamed by Orphic song; and those who follow dancing in his wake are apes.

Kleist, also very earnest, replies without thinking: Life is growing increasingly complicated, and trust becoming ever more difficult.

A pause ensues, involving no feeling of embarrassment. Kleist perceives that Günderrode has been listening to them and is pleased. He is not unskilled in the art of conversing with another person indirectly. Now he will tell them a thing or two.

More than once, he says, he has firmly resolved never to return to his native Prussia.

They do not ask why. Their imaginative powers are inadequate to the task of supplying them with the right questions to ask. He is familiar with this reaction. Their unsuspicious minds. What could possibly drive a young Prussian nobleman from an old and distinguished family out of his own country? A country to which, as he himself now says, he is attached against his will. And to which—only a few short years ago!—he gladly sacrificed his youth: something which these gentlemen here can scarcely understand because they are used to living in a region whose borders are constantly shifting and to being ruled by an ever-changing succession of sovereigns. Indeed, it appears that in a short time they will even be ruled by that Foreigner. He, on the other hand—the thought has just occurred to him for the first time—has never lived in a true commonwealth, but rather in his ideal image of a state. Later he intends to pursue this line of thought further and see where it leads.

The first time he crossed the border, he says, he realized that his native land looked better and better to him the farther away from it he got; that he was gradually ceasing to be weighed down by a self-imposed obligation to his country which he could never live up to; and what a relief it was to be able to sleep again, to gain a new sense of vitality. Lying before him he sees Würzburg, Dresden,

Zurich, the little island in the Lake of Thun, even Weimar. The days of inner freedom he experienced there are something he will never know in Berlin.

Suddenly, he says, he found himself able to think something which he had never dreamed possible before: that he ought to pluck the flower of happiness wherever it was to be found. Thus, he said, he had determined to seek out a new homeland, and never would he forget that night...

He breaks off, language forsakes him. As if the organ of speech were setting up obstacles to its own progress, Günderrode thinks, in order to prevent the man from revealing to others more than is good for him. An excessive enthusiasm which imposes restraints on itself. The things the man must have to endure. She takes in him an interest unmixed with pity. Pitying people makes it too easy to see through them, and that bores her.

That night, thinks Kleist. It was December when I entered Switzerland, setting foot on the soil of my new homeland. A quiet, steady rain was falling. I looked for stars among the clouds. Both nearby and far away, everything was so dark. I felt as if I were stepping into a new life.

No one urges him on; they all wait. The Privy Councilor, thinking the pause has lasted long enough, says quietly: And then?

And then? Kleist replies in a sarcastic tone. Can't you imagine what happened? Nowhere have I found what I was seeking.

And that is? This from Merten, who will not drop the matter.

Kleist is silent.

Well, Merten says, he believes he understands. But how could a single individual who is not cut to the measure of the crowd urge his extraordinary aims upon a state, urge those high-flown demands he makes of life on a commonwealth, which, after all, has to satisfy the needs of all —the farmer, the merchant, the courtier—as well as the poet?

As if he had not already racked his soul out of his body over that question. Good! he says vehemently. If the state rejects the demands I place upon it, let it reject me as well. If only it could convince me that it does in fact satisfy the needs of the farmer and the merchant: that it does not compel all of us to subjugate our higher aims to its interests. The crowd, it's called. Am I fraudulently to transform my aims and views to accord with theirs? And above all the question remains: What would really benefit this crowd in the first place? But no one poses this question. Not in Prussia.

Kleist, my good man! cries Savigny. What deep waters are you heading for?

Yes, it's true, say Kleist. Many things which people consider worthy of veneration are not so to me. Much of what to them appears contemptible is not so to me. I bear an inner precept inscribed in my heart, compared to which all external maxims, were they sanctioned by a king himself, are of no value whatever.

My God, man! Savigny exclaims. You reel all that off like a drill sergeant repeating military regulations. Aren't you afraid? Do you really feel no fear?

There is no possible answer to that question. Fear. If only you knew, my dear man: nameless fear. Often I think that I was born into the world simply to find a name for this fear. And I am close to finding it, very close. I must lie in ambush for it inside myself. The faces people would make if I tried to tell them that it is my destiny to snap at my own heels trying to catch myself, the way the Privy Councilor's foolish dog snaps at his own tail! If only they could simply concede to an unhappy man the right to be unhappy.

Merten feels compelled to make a comment. Herr von Kleist, if he understands him aright, is trying to express the fact that he feels incapable of accommodating himself to any conventional situation in this world.

Kleist is weary of this empty babble. To be sure, he says, he finds many of this world's institutions so unsuited to his needs that it is impossible for him to participate in the labor of maintaining or developing them further. Wedekind reminds him that, in Prussia, Kleist did after all have some prospect of obtaining a post in the commercial delegation of the civil service.

With Struensee, yes. He was not ill disposed toward me. But are you really aware of the militantly organized structure of the entire system of Prussian commerce? When the minister whose service I was to have entered spoke to me concerning the effective performance of some device, he was not referring, let us say, to its effectiveness in mathematical terms—a subject on which I might have had something to say. No. By the effective performance of a device, he meant quite simply the amount of money it would bring in.

Joseph Merten can only laugh at that. But, my dear man, the effects of a device in mathematical terms are of interest only to the degree that they produce an economic effect.

Am I mad? Or are they? One day things will reach such a pass that even the children on the street will make fun of me for my ignorance of the world. It has already gotten so bad that I no longer dare so much as utter a word like "truth."

If things are as you say, why then does the government spend millions on all these institutions for the dissemination of learning? Is the state concerned with truth? The state? A state recognizes no other value than that which can be reckoned in terms of percentages. It desires to know truth only to the extent that it can make use of it. What for? For arts and trades. But arts are not something that one can extort from people, like the manifestation of military skills. If the arts and sciences do not help themselves, no king will come to their aid. All that they can desire of kings is that their natural course of development not be interfered with.

Such ideas, Kleist! says Brentano, dismayed. To whom can you possibly confide them back there in Berlin?

No one, says Kleist. Not one single human soul. And as I have little skill in artfulness and craft, I have learned to keep silent. A demanding but rewarding art. I advise you to cultivate it. The Corsican stands just outside your door.

A real slip of the tongue, that: he ought not to have created this sense of oppression. The Privy Councilor comes to the rescue: Then you have no course open to you, Kleist, but to make a wealthy match!

You're right. Too bad for me, for the most part the nobility of Brandenburg are completely impoverished. What choice is left? It's a toss of the dice. France or Prussia. A civil-service post or a literary career. Degradation with a modest income, or naked poverty with one's pride left intact.

They are unable to take that seriously. They laugh, wave their arms, go over to join the ladies. Savigny takes Kleist's arm. I don't want to hurt your feelings, Kleist, he says. But I fancy that you view your situation as just sufficiently hopeless as you need to in order to ensure that it overwhelms you.

So now he is being accused of luxuriating in suffering? That was all he needed. If only they suspected how he would like to luxuriate in pleasure. How he would like to live among cheerful people as one of their own, pursuing an occupation which enabled him to earn a living without at the same time turning him into a wreck. But how can this man know that, in God's whole wide world, this simple happiness does not exist for him?

Let's drop the subject, he says to Savigny. Don't hold my behavior against me. God knows, and believe me I know too, that often one has no choice but to commit some wrong, either against others or against oneself. And that one must somehow come to terms with this fact, and understand that it is the way of the world.

In the gentle afternoon light streaming in through the windows, they all gather again around the big table.

Günderrode longs to be in the free and open air outdoors. She would like to allow peacefully to ripen within her those ideas which came to her during her conversation with Bettine; but Lisette draws her aside. Lisette, the clever, educated one, with her Romance languages, her botanical studies, her yen for poetry, and that gaze which is always and exclusively fastened on her husband, Nees von Esenbeck, the lean blithe man whose sickliness is a perpetual source of concern and a grave reproach to his wife.

Not mincing words, she tells Günderrode that she considers it unseemly for her to have secret conferences with Bettine in front of everyone this way.

Jealousy? Tears? Lisette! If there was anywhere a happy woman, I thought you were she.

And that is in fact true, Lisette insists, as far as Nees is concerned. But it is also true that the circumstances of domestic life are bound to make a woman unhappy. The suppressed passions . . . This, from her? Günderrode marvels. People know nothing of each other.

Lisette reproaches her with having forgotten everything there once was between them. How, in the evenings, she often used to come to sit beside Günderrode in the latter's room at the convent and have intimate chats with her. How she, Lisette, had fled from an uninteresting visitor and waited for Günderrode at the postern gate of the convent—as if I were your sweetheart, Lina, and we were having a love affair. How we kissed each other when you came out. It was very dark except for the narrow sickle of the moon on the horizon, and there was a fragrance of jasmine in the air.

Günderrode does not recall the incident, but says nothing. As if the years were transparent, she sees the present-day and the old Lisette standing side by side, and one of them knows nothing of the other. Change is unrelenting, and I, she thinks, would prefer not to have to go through it.

Then the moment of intimacy is past. In this narrow circle Lisette is actually forced to stress her status as a married woman. She exaggerates her concern for Nees, asking that the window be closed because drafts are not good for him. It is a kind of revenge when the wife who is not allowed to assume a prominent role herself turns her husband into a child. I cannot talk with her about it, Günderrode thinks. The openness which used to exist between us is a thing of the past. Soon she, too, will decide that I am arrogant.

It is a bad habit to appraise one's friends with the eyes of one taking leave of them forever. Worse still to be compelled to imagine what they will say to each other, once it has come to pass, concerning one's imminent death.

Arrogance. In her heart of hearts, where she is ruthless in self-judgment, Günderrode knows that this reproach is not so far off the mark, even if, like most reproaches, it does not get down to the core of the matter. Arrogant, that she is. Just a little while ago, when she was sitting with Bettine in the window alcove and Bettine was speaking to her in her animated way about the genius of the inconsequential, it dawned on Günderrode how necessary this genius was to her, and how necessary Bettine was to her, in enabling her to dissolve, over and over, that secret feeling of superiority which has always cut her off from other people. The inconsequential! Bettine does not suspect how this word has preyed on her ever since, for the first time, it appeared in one of her letters. Now she is saying, impudently and not without an air of triumph, to Lisette and the Servière girls, to Gunda and Sophie, that Günderrode intends to be her disciple in inconsequentiality, and that the two of them have shaken hands on the deal. There is, she says, a secret pact between them, and she cannot give away more than that.

Then everyone begins to scold Bettine, saying that all she will achieve by this pact will be to set up obstacles to Günderrode's systematic studies, instead of finally accommodating herself to having her own mind properly trained. Bettine makes a wry face and hardly bothers to defend herself. Günderrode is still immersed in her musings about that word—inconsequentiality. How it forces its way into her fantasies of her own importance, fantasies whose existence she scarcely confesses to herself. And how it helps her to rend asunder the web of deceit which hides her from herself. She intends to publish her new poems and dramatic efforts under another name; she will obey the urge to remain incognito. She perceives too clearly how the expectations of the public are imposing constraints on her. On the other hand, how many things become easy and natural for her, and how much closer she comes to other people, when she ceases to wish to be a person of consequence.

The afternoon has given her what was in its power to give. Now she would like to leave.

Kleist knows these groups of people who get together merely so that their members can confirm one another in their views. He has fixed and, as he believes, well-grounded views concerning the education of women, and he has had occasion to test them on his own sisters and on the women of the Zenge household. He has tasted to the full the voluptuousness of teaching others: should a man aim to perform all right actions, or must he be satisfied if all his actions are right? A mental exercise. Good heavens! Had he not heard a secret titter behind his back when he said that?

Now what's going on? It's true, Clemens Brentano is preparing to read a poem aloud, and Günderrode, who is the butt of this tactic, is unable to dissuade him. The man intends to use her own verses as evidence against her. He is calling the assembled company to bear witness that the poet Tian has proved guilty of inconsistency.

A verse dialogue, almost everyone here appears familiar with it. Someone named Violetta is accusing someone else, appropriately called Narcissus, of being inconstant in love. Thereupon Narcissus replies:

To me that is not constancy which you call constancy.
To me that is not inconstant which is so to you!
He who divides the moment of supreme life,
Not forgetting, but blissfully abiding in his love,

Who continues to judge, to calculate, to measure,
Him I call inconstant, he is not to be trusted,
His cold consciousness will lucidly gaze through you,
The judge of your forgetfulness of self.
But I am faithful! Everything, my whole being,
Will be filled to the brim by the object
To which I yield myself in the bonds of love.

The recitation is refuting rather than proving Clemens's point; he feels this himself. The quality of the silence has altered. Kleist is hyper-alert. That she should dare, that she should deliver herself over into the hands of other people. The woman must be mad. In her anger she is also beautiful.

Clemens, says Günderrode, there is no way I can fight the obtuse reviewers. But how then am I to fight a friend who deliberately sets out to hurt me?

Clemens, red-faced, asks her forgiveness. Finally he is being himself, without dissimulation. The matter seems to have been settled. Kleist has never before been among people who trespass so greatly on each other's territory and yet do not become enemies as a result. A glimmer of hope that certain dreams of his young manhood, of which he now feels ashamed, might conceivably come true after all: trust might not be an absurdity, love not a phantasm. But he does not want to turn soft. To Günderrode, who happens to be standing beside him, he says that he finds it significant that she should have put those concluding lines of her poem in the future tense. Yes, she says, that's true. It only just struck me for the first time.

While Clemens was reading, Günderrode had experienced a sensation familiar to her from a walk she took along the edge of a swamp, when she trod on a piece of boggy turf. Suddenly the ground gave way beneath her like a drum on which the skin has not been drawn taut. She felt intense joy mingled with intense dread. Her friends, panic-stricken, drew her back onto firm ground, told her she was reckless. She said nothing in reply. Not reckless but curious, yes, that she is to be sure—curious about the moment when the ground gives way beneath one's feet. It is a craving of that obdurate, heinous kind which is rightly forbidden to us by a prohibition so binding that the others, the Ten Commandments, pale in comparison. To slay one's father and one's mother: evil, but something that can be atoned for. But to destroy *oneself*: that is monstrous, against nature. She is forced to struggle against her conscience. The resistance is growing stronger.

If only we could find peace!

It is inglorious, Kleist is thinking, to allow oneself to be broken by the times in which one lives. Why, why should I not be able to live with these people here.

There are days like these which never come to an end. The clock strikes five, people decide to go outdoors. Kleist, already breathing a sigh of relief, and hoping for a walk in the fresh air unmolested by other people, is instead forced to undergo a cross-examination by Merten. The merchant, although naturally a mere reader incompetent to judge matters of literary technique, nevertheless cannot refrain from warning the young author against continuing to produce works of the contrived and artificial nature of his first play.

This is the tone that turns Kleist mute. He refuses to say that he himself regards the Schroffenstein play as sheer trash. He stammers something about passions which dominate the lives of men and do not care a straw for logic.

Once again Merten cannot help smiling. Did not the greatness of our present age consist precisely in the fact that it had curbed the baser passions and elevated reason to a position of power? Clemens asks whether, in this case, Merten requires of a literary composition the same order and clarity which reign among his account books, and Merten ingenuously replies: Well, why not? Why should not the rules which have proved their worth in one discipline also be valid in another. To which Kleist, under the sway of the compulsion to discuss a topic from all possible angles, comes back with: Order! Yes. Today the world is indeed orderly. But tell me, is it still beautiful?

That would depend on one's concept of beauty. —The man is not only exacting, the man is right. And contrary to all expectation, he even proves able to cite a line from the drama of his honored guest, as an example of an aberration in the concept of beauty: "Ah!—the moment after a crime is often the most beautiful moment in human life." Did not this line in fact almost amount to an appeal by the poet to commit a crime?

Kleist casts a strained glance into the merchant's gray eyes. No chance of striking the slightest spark there. Languidly he justifies the disputed line, meanwhile wondering whether his defense is at all valid. It is love, he hears himself saying, which is trying to grasp at some consolation . . .

Grinding out the same old empty chatter he has learned by heart. Why not simply walk with quiet attention along this narrow little street between the low, half-timbered houses, before which old women sit gossiping and knitting. Why this desire to always prove one's point?

Bettine announces that the only law to which people must subject themselves is that of the unfettered, unbounded—but not irresponsible!—enjoyment of life.

Kleist, out of sorts, counters: No. One must first have passed through the school of the sciences before one is allowed to scorn them.

The sciences? Which are in the process of forging iron bands around our hearts and our heads? Which are paving the way to an iron century in which art will find itself standing outside with the doors closed in its face, and the artist will be an alien in the world?

Once again this synchronization among them. There's only one little touch still missing: that someone should mention the word "progress."

Lisette takes over this role right on cue. Rousseau's renowned study of whether progress in science and art has exercised a pernicious or a beneficent effect on manners.

Oh yes, we all know everything.

Kleist has a vision of an age founded on empty talk rather than actions. The landscape around him is swallowed up in a sober light. And there we are, still sitting there, and acting on the basis of the catch phrases of the century before, splitting hairs and struggling against our weariness, which keeps gaining ground on us, and all the time knowing: this is not anything we could live or die for. Our blood will be shed, and no one will tell us why.

Kleist feels in himself a violence which arouses terror as well as joy.

The path of science has separated from that of art, he says rather lamely. Our modern-day civilization is steadily expanding the sphere of the intellect, steadily restricting that of imagination. We have almost reached the point at which we can predict the end of the arts.

As a scientist, Nees von Esenbeck feels he is being personally attacked. In response he does not merely speak but lectures: On the contrary, I believe that the spirit of the age, with its emphasis on scientific progress, simply regards as unimportant the lamentations of the literati, which, understandable as they may be, are also marked by hypochondria. Don't take it personally, my dear Kleist. As for me personally, I would give everything I have in exchange for the chance to live again on this earth two or three centuries from now, and to share in the paradisiac conditions which—thanks to the advance of the sciences! —mankind will then enjoy.

There is a flaw underlying this thinking, but it is still too early to give it a name. These views of yours, says Kleist, are not based on a comprehensive vision, a vision of the totality of things, but on the primacy of individual disciplines. Am I then to devote all my faculties, all my energies, my whole life, simply to learn to know one single class of insects, or to assign a plant to its proper place in the scheme of things? Must mankind pass through this desert in order to arrive at the Promised Land? I cannot believe that it is so. Alas, how sad it is, this unilateral, cyclopean view of things!

What solution do you propose? This from Savigny, whose voice everyone has been waiting to hear. Should we close down all the laboratories? Prohibit the further development of any apparatus which serve the advancement of research? Suppress our noblest impulse, curiosity?

Savigny, says Günderrode, Savigny sees everything in terms of Either-Or. You must know, Kleist, he has a masculine brain. He knows only one kind of curiosity: curiosity concerning that which is incontrovertible, logically consistent, and soluble.

This woman. As if she had some special intimation of the hidden contradiction on which the ruination of mankind is predicated. And as if she could somehow summon up the strength, not to deny this rift, but to endure it.

But, cries Merten, it is not the poet's mission to deprive his fellow man of all hope!

By God, Herr Merten, you're right there. The poet's charge is the administration of our illusions.

Now, on top of everything else, they will think he is being ironical. Where are we all headed? Man has an irresistible need for enlightenment, for without enlightenment he is not much more than an animal. But as soon as we set foot in the realm of knowledge, an evil magic appears to turn against us whatever application we make of our knowledge. Thus, in the end, regardless of whether we are enlightened or ignorant, we have lost as much as we have gained.

What do you mean, exactly?

Kleist answers Günderrode: In other words, man, like Ixion, is damned to trundle a wheel up a mountain, which, each time that it reaches the halfway point, plunges back into the abyss. How unfathomable is that will which rules over the human race. Can God demand responsibility from such beings as we are?

Kleist, very wrought up by the conversation—how swiftly he loses his equanimity!—tells the Privy Councilor, while hammering both fists against his skull: Yes, yes, yes! Perhaps this is where the flaw lies. In the fact that nature was so cruel as to lay my brain out wrong, so that no matter which path my mind embarks on, it encounters absurdity standing and grinning at it. Wedekind, if you are really a doctor: open up my skull! Look and find out where the flaw is. Take your scalpel and, without trembling, cut out the perverted place. It may be that what I read in the faces of my family is true: that I am an abortive genius, a kind of monster. Doctor, I implore you: operate on me, remove the abortion. None of the patients you have healed by your art will be more grateful to you than I.

My good man! Günderrode hears Wedekind say in an unaccustomed tone. What are you thinking of!

Whereupon Kleist replies, calm but exhausted: That which can be thought ought to be thought. Do you not believe that too, Privy Councilor?

Out of the courtyards float the sounds of simple labor, the blows of axes, the clanking of buckets. Chickens along the path, which at the end of the street opens out to the pastureland along the shore. Earth under one's feet. The sky on one's shoulders. The dainty little houses, which draw together slightly in their hostility to him. The conspiracy of objects.

Talk, talk.

Savigny. Talking about the equivocal, challengeable aspects of the poet's existence. The fact that the poet never has to put anything he says into practice, inasmuch as he invents his own world, including the obstacles in it, and thus always deals solely with the reflections thrown off by his own imagination.

Kleist thinks—but takes care not to say aloud— Of all the people here, perhaps there is none more intimately bound to the real world than I am. Appearances are deceptive. Then Günderrode says, as if she were speaking in his name: People who are not deceived about themselves will extract something fresh out of the foment of every age, simply by lending it expression. I feel that the world could not go on if this were not done.

So she would see the abysm of time as the crater of a volcano, asks Savigny.

I like that image, says Günderrode. Clemens, who now moves to the head of the group, turns around: Last night I dreamed that Goethe was dead. While I was dreaming, I wept myself almost blind.

A tempest breaks loose, as if Clemens had not spoken about a dream but about a real event. Kleist is forced to suppress a twinge of jealousy, as if only he were allowed to dream of Goethe—which, by the way, he never does. Actually, this amazes him.

Günderrode, who has remained at his side, has just re-read Goethe's *Tasso*. "I feel as if all my bones were shattered deep inside me, and I am alive simply in order to feel this."

Yes, he too could cite a few apropos verses. On the proper scale of talent in relation to life, an up-to-date theme. And yet he had felt some doubt as to whether the author had succeeded in drawing the ultimate consequences from the relationships between his characters.

What did he mean exactly.

In a moment he will be confessing to this woman that thing which so far he has told no one—and he knows why.

It offends me that Tasso's dissension with the Prince should be based on a misapprehension. How would it be if it were not Tasso who committed an injustice against the Prince, and especially Antonio, but rather they against him? What if his misfortune were not imaginary but real and ineluctable? If it were not eccentric enthusiasm but a keen, or let us say overly keen, sense of the true state of affairs which wrung from him that cry: "Whither wend I my step in order to flee the loathing which howls about me, to escape the abyss which lies before me?" —You are smiling, Günderrode?

Keep talking.

The Privy Councilor of Weimar, I think, has no particular penchant for tragedy, and I believe I know why.

Out with it then.

He is concerned with harmony. He believes that those contrary forces which are active in the world can be divided into two branches of reason—he calls them good and evil—both of which, ultimately, make an essential contribution to the progress of mankind.

And you, Kleist?

I? Suddenly Kleist perceives what distinguishes him from that Other; the thing which will always make him inferior and the other man unassailable.

I am unable to divide the world into good and evil, into two branches of reason, into healthy and sick. If I wanted to divide the world, I should have to turn the ax on myself, cleave my inner self in twain and offer the two halves to the disgusted public so that they would have good cause to wrinkle up their noses and say: Whatever has happened to wholesome entertainment? Yes indeed, what I have to put on display is unclean. Not something you would bite into and swallow down. Something to make you run away, Günderrode.

After they have taken a few more steps, he picks up a dry stick and with rapid, nimble strokes traces a figure in the sandy path, a sort of absurd geometrical construction, a mechanical device gone awry. This, he said, was his blueprint for a tragic drama. He would like to know what she thinks of this impossible object, the presupposition of which is that, once it is set into motion, it is condemned to destroy itself.

Günderrode, who has never in her life seen, or even thought of, anything like it, understands it at once.

Well? Kleist asks. His lips tremble. You know it yourself, the woman says. This is no tragic play. This is Fate. A pronouncement which appears to gratify the stranger in some remarkable way. They walk along in silence. Once Kleist politely takes Karoline's arm. Little walls of natural stone running along before apple orchards past the time of blossoms; narrow vineyards; a world without a single false note. They pass by tiny windows on a level with their heads. Blooming red geraniums, blinding-white curtains puffed out by the breeze, in front of dark rooms with their insoluble enigmas. Now and then, looking as if it were terror-stricken, a flat pale face framed by a close-fitting cap.

The Privy Councilor of Weimar, says Kleist, and Herr Merten, as well, praise the virtues of the new age as opposed to the old. But I, Günderrode, I and you as well, I think, are suffering from the evils of the new age.

From the yards and the cellar windows there streams all year long the odor of fermenting wine. Günderrode says that she rarely drinks wine. As a rule she must pay for the pleasure with a headache. She verifies for Kleist that at this time the adults are in fact still working in the vineyards. Only old people and children gaze, without wonder, after the strolling party. The last habitation before they reach the riverbank pastures is a carpentry shop. Gleaming white wood stacked up in the yard. The trenchant sound of a saw. I quite understood your desire to become a carpenter, says Günderrode. I, too, should like to sit around a table with other people in the evening after a day of simple labor. The warmth. The nearness of others.

He says that it was not the evening table which had inspired this desire in him, or the circle of candlelight. It was a chair which he had seen at Wedekind's home, which had made him feel that he had never really looked at a chair before. A beautiful piece, solid, durable. Then, he says, it seemed to me so natural to devote skill and energy and industry to the manufacture of furniture like this, whose usefulness is beyond question.

Yes, says Günderrode, it is quite understandable that we attempt to flee the coercion to which we are subject, at least in our thoughts. In the real world we are not permitted to do so.

Was she failing to take him seriously enough? Or taking him too seriously? And what gave her the right to sum up the two of them, both herself and him, in the word "we"?

Bettine, who seems to know everyone and is darting back and forth among the various groups, catches up with them, and in a mischievous frame of mind asks what they would wish for if they had three wishes and could wish for anything they liked. Günderrode laughs: I'll tell you later. She knows of no wish she could make, her wishes are boundless.

And you, Kleist?

Kleist says: Freedom. A poem. A home.

Irreconcilable things which you want to reconcile.

Yes, he says lightly. I know.

Bettine promises them an extraordinarily beautiful sunset. She besieges Clemens, whose guitar she has carried after him, to sing them all something. Good, he says, just one song, his most recent. Dedicated to Tian, the beautiful poet. He sings:

Sweet May, young man of blossoms,
Bring her peace offerings: blooming boughs.
Ask her, sweet-tongued,
To show you the flower
Which she would willingly trust
To gaze into her bosom.
And then I will to the meadows
And pluck her a pleasant wreath,
Teaching the flowers to say:
"Would that grace would show indulgence to guilt,
Which already has suffered harsh punishment."

A magic emanates from Clemens which reconciles one to his bad habits, even though she knows that this is exactly what he intends it to do. Kneeling, he hands her a tree bough. She puts up with it, plays the gracious sovereign. Everyone applauds and demands new songs. Come, Kleist, says Günderrode, taking his arm and drawing him along the path leading upstream, while the rest of the company turns onto the right-hand path along the shore. At once she regrets having done so. She ought to have suppressed the impulse. He, too, would prefer to walk alone. He curses the strict indoctrination, which prevents him from withdrawing from others whenever he chooses. For what purpose has he spent all these desolate winter months in Mainz, if they have not afforded him a little measure of freedom in his dealings with others?

Günderrode says to herself, but as if she were replying to him: Yes, it has been her most painful experience to learn that only that within us which wishes to be destroyed is destructible; that only that can be seduced which meets seduction halfway; that only that can be free which is capable of freedom; that this realization conceals itself, in the most monstrous fashion, from the person to whom it is of the greatest moment; and that the battles we exhaust ourselves in fighting are often no more than shadow-boxing that takes place in our minds.

It occurs to Kleist to wonder whether he could have suffered so much because of a simple mistake. Accustomed as he is to being cruel to himself, this thought gives him a fierce joy in which he would gladly immerse himself wholly. This, for once, would really constitute an idea that could kill a man if he simply took it to heart; but there is the Fräulein, glancing over at him, dexterously set into the landscape, a cheap theatrical trick, awkward and exasperating. Kleist makes no attempt to conceal the fact that he sees through this contrivance. Then again he is disturbed by the fact that he feels this need to make a conscious decision about his slightest impulse. Authentic actions spring directly from the soul, without first passing through the head, but he is incapable of such acts—a matter he had often discussed with Pfuel to the point of exhaustion.

Now he suddenly understands his perpetual weariness. An image occurs to him: a machine which is made to run at full speed while at the same time the brake is being applied. The wear and tear must be considerable, even calculable. It is, he says, extremely singular how, after recognizing that a certain way of thinking is wrong, one nevertheless succumbs to it over and over, and cannot summon the strength to force the cart out of its rut. Frequently, an external shock will come to the aid of the mind bogged down in its habits, as happened to him several years ago in Butzbach when the horses pulling his coach, terrified by the braying of a donkey somewhere behind them, ran away and placed him and his sister in extreme peril.

Butzbach? says Günderrode. But I know it so well. My grandmother lived there, and after she died I lived there for six months!

Kleist describes to her the place where the accident occurred. She is able to supplement his account with many details which he did not notice in the heat of the moment. But never will he forget that skeptical thought which he had believed would be his last thought in life. So, a human life is dependent on the braying of an ass?

Now I feel as if I were responsible for that thought of yours, merely because it occurred to you in Butzbach! cries Günderrode, laughing.

You believe then, says Kleist, that there is something substantial which we can use to combat the blind chance which governs our lives!

She is touched by the man. She does not know whether or not she likes him, but even if she were to take a distinct dislike to him, it would not cloud her judgment of him. This is the quality in her which other people call her coldness—her refusal to abandon herself to her prejudices. Besides, she does not wish to impose her views on Herr von Kleist, who, precisely when he grows most vehement and earnest, has something strange about him, although she could not define its nature and extent. She must get together with Bettine and think over the question of why she so frequently encounters young men to whom she feels superior.

Your question, Kleist, leads to nothing but self-torture. The donkey brayed, your horse ran away—well and good. Your pride rebels against the idea of such a death. But could you really have called it accidental? Would it not have represented the consequence of events which you yourself put into motion? What impelled you to go to Butzbach? What were you seeking on this journey which you were free to choose not to make?

You are very perspicacious, Günderrode. That journey —it was very strange, from the outset it was governed by two stars. In part I *wanted* to make it in order to seek diversion, for, through more intimate acquaintance with the philosophy of Kant, I had lost my only and highest ideal—the acquisition of truth and the cultivation of the mind—for now it appeared to me impossible to achieve knowledge. Yet in part the journey was also *imposed* upon me. My sister did not wish to relinquish her participation in my lot, so in order for her to accompany me, we had to obtain other papers recording the goal and purpose of our undertaking. What was I to say to the authorities? Then suddenly there was "Paris" written on my papers, and to my astonishment and incredulity: "For the study of mathematics and natural science." I, who had nothing in mind but to flee all knowledge! My portfolio was already full of letters of recommendation addressed to scholars in the French capital. I thought I was dreaming. Ought I really to make the journey? Did I still want to? Was it still permissible for me to back out? Thus, my power of free choice was secretly rendered counterfeit, I was unable to extricate myself from the tangle, and it was with the most ambivalent feelings that I climbed into the coach to travel to Paris.

Viewed in this light, he thinks, adding a mental footnote, that incident in Butzbach would in fact be nothing less than an unmotivated, random chance. In retrospect, he almost approves this game for those about to be executed, which, employing threads of the most diverse order —those which it takes up without a purpose, by sheer inadvertence, as well as those involving fatality or compulsion—skillfully weaves them together in order to lay a trap for a man.

It cheers him up when he can catch life up to its little tricks.

Now he is silent once again. Günderrode cannot decide what subjects relating to his life she dare talk about with him, and which not. Of course she will not mention the parson's daughter from Wiesbaden, concerning whom she has heard malicious whispers from Wedekind. This man Kleist does not look to be the type one could compliment on his amorous conquests. That, indeed, is a point in his favor. Fortunately, although her strict self-control has been relaxed by her weariness and by Savigny's presence, she thinks of a negligible incident which, of all the casual gossip she has heard about Kleist, had been the one thing that arrested her attention.

Your sister, I hear, is an enterprising lady?

In what sense, enterprising?

Why this same old touchiness. Why does he still, and as he knows full well, why will he always, until the end of his days, feel this vulnerability at the mere mention of his family. Once a knife has cut deep into the flesh, a feather, touching the same spot, gives one pain. He cannot, by main force, bring about that one thing which alone would relieve the pain: either to love in return, as they deserve, those people among whom he found all that is capable of captivating a heart—love, trust, indulgence, support both in word and in deed—or to confess to himself that it is not possible for him to do so, and thus to free himself of guilt. So action and feeling run counter to each other within me . . .

Your sister, they say, accompanied you to Paris dressed in man's clothing. He is incapable of perceiving the more profound interest underlying Günderrode's questions. She is like all the rest. Interested in the sensational, nothing more. Ulrike, poor girl.

Günderrode can read his thoughts and feels herself blush. She makes no effort to conceal from him the irritation she feels, and which he so richly deserves, as he regales her with that anecdote he has successfully tried out on so many people, and which centers on Ulrike: how, when she was in Paris, where no one else perceived that this person dressed in man's clothing was really a woman, she was addressed as "Madame" by a blind musician whom she had complimented on his artistry, and had then had to leave the salon with Kleist as if they were fleeing for their lives.

Günderrode does not laugh. She rarely feels envy, but she is feeling it now.

I wish I knew your sister.

Kleist wonders: ought he to feel offended? He asks her the reason for her wish.

Günderrode is indifferent as to whether she is speaking with a narrow- or a liberal-minded man. She says that, from what she has observed, the lives of women require more courage than those of men. When she hears about a woman who has managed to summon up this necessary courage, she very much wants to know her. For things have reached such a pass that women—even women who are far removed from each other in many respects—must lend each other support, since men were no longer capable of doing so.

She must explain that to him in more detail.

Oh, Kleist, you know perfectly well what I mean. It's because the men for whom we might care are themselves entangled in inextricable dilemmas. The constant round of responsibilities you men must deal with cut you into pieces which scarcely bear any relation to each other. We women are looking for a whole human being, and we cannot find him.

Now the man is silent. Ought a woman to speak in this manner? What, in any case, is forcing him to discuss the appointed role of her sex and his with this woman whom he has just met for the first time in his life and will never see again? What is forcing him to talk about his most deeply concealed self-doubt, the most distressing of his failures? That matter which remains unspeakable?

As far as Ulrike is concerned, Fräulein Günderrode, with that empathy sometimes possessed by women, may have the right instinct about her. But he avoids, and intends to continue to avoid, any deeper inquiry into the meaning of that pride, or rather arrogance, which his sister has often displayed. He knows nothing more, and chooses to know nothing more, than the fact that the image of her brother is inscribed in the very foundation of her soul—that brother for whom she took the place of a mother, whom she loves with an exclusive, all-possessive love, and whom she wishes—or is it he who wishes it?—to remain the only man in her life. So she considers him unfeeling? And what if he should insult her by showing her just how considerate he could be? Everything, or almost everything she says and does, fits the picture of a sister who is quite content to make sacrifices for her brother. She, who was not endowed with wealth or property, is not extremely prepossessing nor strikingly charming and feminine—unlike the woman who is now walking at his side—and could scarcely hope to make a good marriage. But who in any case, as far as Kleist can tell, has never set much store by this possibility.

This is the insoluble residue which does not fit into the overall diagram. This is the thing concerning which they cannot and must not ever, with a single word, with even so much as a single glance, show each other that they understand their own and one another's feelings. He not wholly a man, she not wholly a woman . . . But what does that mean, that love between a brother and a sister which human beings cover up that they may not see.

Which they tolerate by failing to perceive what their blood is urging deep down in its abysmal muteness. The benefaction of blood kinship, a thought that is never thought through to the end. A kinship which mitigates one's incomprehension of that alien sex to which one cannot surrender oneself.

Kleist has reason to suspect that even when his engagement to Fräulein von Zenge was in full flower—the longed-for security of the conventional!—Ulrike had had a secret understanding with him regarding the factitious nature of his relationship with his fiancée, which was as irksome to him as her incessant urging that he finally honor his pledge to marry Wilhelmine. Those who know us best know just where to hurt us. Of course, it was not really this prodding on her part which further embittered their sojourn in Paris, which had roused him to a frenzy of rage against her. What really incensed him was the fact that he could not simply rip her farcical playacting to shreds with a single coarse and candid word.

Females.

What you were thinking just now—it was something that you never realized before, wasn't it?

What are you trying to do to me?

He glances around. The yellow of the dandelion amid the green: colors which one would have to bring all the painters in the world to see in order to teach them the true meaning of words like "yellow" and "green." A meadow, too exemplary of all meadows even to be called a meadow. On the right the silvery shimmer of the pastureland, along the riverbank, the reflections from the water playing over their surface. Something within us resists the perfection of nature, in its contrast to our own inner strife.

Günderrode is once more impelled to screen her eyes from the light. Kleist would not wish to be walking alone at this moment. But then again he resents the fact that this woman is expressing a sensation with which he is familiar. Nothing, she says, could be more solid and more beautiful and more real than this landscape, which often seems to her like the extension of herself. And yet in the blink of an eye it could change into a painted canvas stretched over a frame, for no other reason than to mock her. And she was afraid, but at the same time she also desired, that the canvas would tear asunder. When she was sleeping, she would suddenly start up, and she could often hear the sound of the tearing. And what we would see then, Kleist, if we looked through the rents into the abyss behind the beauty: that would turn us mute.

The unwholesome joy of pointing out the levers and gears behind the scenes: Kleist has never before encountered this trait in a woman.

The hideous chaos, she says, the disconnected elements in nature and in us. The barbarous impulses which, more than we know, determine our actions. Not only hideous but hideously real—that she could well imagine.

Such words. Never would the generation preceding them have used such words in a line of theirs.

Both of them are thinking the same name: Goethe.

The most hideous thing, says Kleist, is that inner commandment which compels me to take action against myself.

And Günderrode replies, in the tone in which one quotes a line of poetry: To give birth to what slays me.

He has no way of knowing that she has written lines like this.

Günderrode! Take back what you said.

No, Kleist. We cannot reclaim a single word.

What was it that Wedekind had urged upon him? Moderation, thinking things through carefully, modesty in his demands. Not this tumult. Not the ice-cold hands, the pounding of the pulse in his temples. Not this ticklish pleasure in peril. And not, once again, this unbridled feeling of hope: not any of the things which make him the person he is. Lost, Wedekind. There's nothing to be done about it.

Günderrode, he says, but are we not commanded to stop before such sentences form within us!

Yes, the woman says. We are so commanded.

And?

And we must break the commandment.

Why?

That we never know.

There are birds here which rise up from a tall willow tree, uttering a terrible cry, as they pass by. Kleist starts in alarm. Günderrode places her hand on his arm. They both know that they do not want to be touched. At the same time they feel a pity, a compassion for the repressed language of their bodies, a mourning for the all too precocious taming of their limbs by the military uniform and the religious habit, for the morality in the name of regulations, for the secret excesses they commit in the name of breaking the regulations. One must first be beside oneself in order to know the longing to tear off one's clothing and roll around in this meadow.

Once—it was on his return journey, in disgrace, from the French coast, when even the prospect of death lay in ruins around him—Kleist, at midnight, weary but with overkeen senses, was walking through a gently undulating landscape. When he was in the hollow of the incline, the hills lay about him like the backs of great warm animals, he saw them breathing; he stood still and felt the heart of the earth beating under the soles of his feet, and he gathered his strength in order to endure the sight of the heavens. For the stars—not mere lights, the lights for which he had always taken them before—in their glittering enormous corporeality were threatening to cascade down upon him. He forgot himself without abandoning himself, he ran for a long time, and finally at the right he saw the dawning lights of a village. He knocked at a door, a woman opened it, her face seemed beautiful to him in the candlelight, she let him in, mutely placed a bowl of milk before him on the rough table, and showed him to a bed of straw. He stretched out and experienced in body and limbs what freedom is, without a word even once entering his mind. A measure had been set for him which he had to strive to fulfill—a promise that in man, and even in him, it was possible·to find a path which led into a free and open space. For what we are capable of desiring must lie within the scope of our powers, he thought, or it is not God who rules the world but Satan, and he in a fit of delirium has created a disordered being whose destiny it is, by the sweat of his brow, to pull his own perdition out of the womb of time on a chain forged by unhallowed beings.

His gaze meets that of Günderrode. Now he regrets that he does not know her poetry. It might be worthwhile to measure her unconditional absolutism against his own. Perhaps there is in fact one person under the sun to whom he can confide the affliction which is eating him alive. One cannot understand what one does not share with others.

Goethe, he says, feeling surprised at himself, has, if I am not mistaken, not produced any real poetry for a long time.

She laughs with deep appreciation.

Often, he says, I have even suspected that he—I can't find the word straight off—that he is out of touch with real life.

What do you mean? Something like the lamentation of Leonora Sanvitale, asking why nature did not make Tasso the poet and Antonio the statesman a single human being?

Yes, exactly! cries Kleist. Something like that. —He had stopped stammering some time ago. —The fact that he regards what is absolutely impossible as desirable, and therefore as within our power to bring about.

But, after all, he tried out his theory on his own life and found that it worked.

And undoubtedly he paid the price for it.

The innumerable hours he has spent trying to come to terms with this man, blind with love and keen-eyed with hatred. Feeling a presentiment of every humiliation which the other man still had in store for him. Madness, thus to drive the thorn deep into one's own flesh. And what about him, that other? What if he came through without a scratch, not threatened in the least by my existence? If I should fail to pay him back for my sufferings. I will tear the laurel from his brow.

Aren't you afraid that the standard to which you have submitted yourself might destroy you?

As a woman, Günderrode, you cannot know the meaning of ambition.

The word has been spoken.

This man, Günderrode thinks, is alien to me, and in his alienness he is close to me. Ambition, she says, as if she were listening carefully to the word.

Do not take this Fury lightly, Günderrode.

Do you want to spend your whole life running, pursued by Furies?

Want to! You make me laugh.

To them it seems an iron necessity.

When I *must* do something, I train myself to want it as well.

And in this way you create for yourself the illusion of freedom.

From what she has observed, she says, the ambition of gifted people is intensified by inauspicious circumstances, the ambition of the untalented by their distorted self-esteem.

Well said. And to which group would you assign me?

Every man knows that about himself.

No, Günderrode! Don't you see many a man build the edifice of his misfortune on a foundation of self-deception? And he doesn't even notice what he's doing, not to save his life?

That's true, she says. Our blindness. The fact that we cannot know where our paths will take us when we wander off the beaten track. It is a law that with time all comprehension of us must fade. But whether those things which we venture to achieve in our lives will, at some later day, achieve a certain validation . . .

Kleist wonders when and how the dark coloration entered his life and spread out there like black ink in a vessel filled with clear water. He remembers—but as if he were remembering a stranger—the Sundays during his term as an officer, when he would travel cross-country from Potsdam with three friends and strike up the dancing music in little country inns. That happened in another lifetime. He has lost even the ability to wish to return to it. —Does this woman beside him, who has mastered the art of keeping silent for a long time, who knows when to let a question drop, see those same refractions of green in the shadows cast by the willows? Does the river, which appears to be virtually standing still, possess for her this same metallic gleam which the sun, by its position relative to the earth, creates only at this hour? Everything has some explanation. He sees himself and her from a long distance away as if, at the same time that he is walking beside her, he were standing at some observation post high above them, and saw them as droll figures on the banks of the Rhine. Not a bad subject for a watercolor. But would a painter be able to capture on paper the separation of each figure from itself, from the other, and from the natural world around it? That is not granted us, thinks Kleist.

And do you also know why the old man in Weimar cannot write a tragedy?

Well, why?

He is afraid. That's why.

She fails to assent, to play the role of accomplice. She says, as if she had been thinking about something else: Kleist, you take life so seriously that it is dangerous.

One day, Günderrode, he will be afraid of me.

How disagreeable for you.

They are silent.

And you, Günderrode? Are you trying to convince yourself that you can reconcile yourself to your restricted existence?

Suddenly he feels afraid. For ages now, he has refrained from trespassing on the forbidden territory of another person's life. Is he feeling threatened, that he is being thus driven to attack?

"Red—the color of life and the color of death." A thought stripped of its context. Günderrode sees herself in the black habit of her order with the stiff high collar, standing, as the youngest member of the order, at the long table, until Mother Superior gives the signal for prayer and then for the beginning of the meal. Her paralysis, her dread of it all. She can clearly hear the sound which screens her off from all ordinary sounds and informs her that it is time to withdraw, to close the curtains and to stretch out on the hard narrow bed. Behind her closed eyelids, to turn dominion over to her headache. The chill of her limbs, the room deathly empty of all sound. The fiery red point above the base of the nose, which vibrates with the beat of her pulse. The retreat of her despised body into itself. And her secret knowledge that she possesses the means to end these days of anguish, but without having to use it yet, because it would hurt more than physical pain ever could to state the reason for her death: To exorcise it, indeed to kill it, by calling it by name. The day on which she would proclaim to herself the name of her sorrow must necessarily be her last day on earth.

"You ardent red, until death my love shall resemble you . . ."

Günderrode, don't speak! Forgive me!

No. Even a confined existence can be expanded until one reaches its outermost limits, which until then are invisible. The only thing lost to us is that which we lack faculties to grasp. Once the eye of the mind has opened, it perceives things invisible to others, which are akin to itself. Everything which stimulates, refreshes, and fulfills the heart is sacred to me, even if no trace of it should persist in the memory.

Is that wisdom, Günderrode? Modesty in one's demands?

Not only the circumstances of my life, but also my own nature, have imposed stricter limitations on my actions than yours have done on you, Kleist.

You have the compensation, the poem. Poems are a luxury which belong only to those favored by fortune.

Among whom you do not count yourself.

No.

It is denied him to express himself directly in a poem. His need to pour out emotion in lines of verse fails to break down the bars placed before certain regions inside him. In the joyous pleasure in life, in his experience of love, and in his poetry, the man from Weimar has outstripped him. A man favored by fortune. Inconceivable, that man, to someone like Kleist—an orphan, almost penniless, and a lieutenant in the garrison at Potsdam, crushed beneath military regulations. Humiliations, the most intolerable of which was to have to humiliate others. That other man has never suffered the pressure of barbarous circumstances like these, such that every dream, even before it was born, was destroyed by the impossibility of its ever being fulfilled, and the vestiges of the dreams decomposed the stuff poems are made of. He does not dare to write them.

Sometimes, says Kleist—something about this woman, like a magnet, draws from him confessions which leave him in the most vulnerable position— Sometimes I find it unendurable that nature has split the human being into man and woman.

You don't mean that, Kleist. What you mean is that man and woman have a hostile relationship inside you. As they do in me.

What does she know of him. What are we getting ourselves into.

We cannot make any predictions.

I am laughing, Günderrode.

Why?

Why does one laugh. Not out of joy. Just as we shall soon cease to weep out of sorrow. Soon we shall have no other response but this laughter to all that is going to befall us. We shall be accompanied by a hellish laughter, I know not where.

We shall not be there, you and I.

No.

If one could understand what kind of current this is that has snatched one up, and how it can carry one away like this. It has a driving force like that of ice floes. It's as if I were standing on an ice floe amid the flowing corridor of ice, in absolute darkness. The river wends I know not whither, the ice floe dips, now to one side, now to the other. And I, pierced through and through with horror, with curiosity, with the dread of death, and with the desire for rest, I must struggle to keep my balance. My whole life long. And you, Günderrode, you tell me now who visits such judgments upon us.

A few people carrying work gear trudge past them, then turn around and look at the man, who has grasped the woman's arm. She seems to see nothing improper in this and appears to need no assistance; nor does she seem concerned about the long distance they must traverse to get back to where they started.

I believe that we are wrong to ask such questions when we confront fate, rather than to see that we are one with fate; that we secretly provoke everything which befalls us. Do you understand, Kleist? If this were not the case, exactly the same thing would happen to everyone who found himself in analogous circumstances.

Could this be the woman of whose love one need have no fear?

One day she would encounter a man of whom she knows nothing. Of whom she can experience nothing, but through whom she will experience herself to the very depths, to her ultimate limits and beyond. And then beyond that there is nothing more. —She recalls when the thought came to her for the very first time: back then, when Savigny climbed into the traveling coach and she jammed his hand in the carriage door; when he was going away, and she, suddenly quite composed, foresaw everything which would follow upon this leave-taking, because it was all sealed and determined within her. She came to understand how many people acquire the gift of clairvoyance: an intense pain or an intense concentration illuminates her inner landscape. Savigny did not appear in it, despite the fact that, she believed, she ardently desired to see him there. It must properly have been her responsibility to nourish and renew a bond, a desire, whose strength and ardor were beginning to flag. But instead she abandoned herself to her indolence, almost her drowsiness. And a short time ago, when, with a large company of guests, she celebrated the wedding of Gunda Brentano and Karl Savigny, she could scarcely shake off the strange sensation that she had already embraced the bride once before, already shaken the bridegroom's hand, already sat before at this same table with the same people and on the same occasion. —She could summon up the inner fire to melt down the wall between herself and the others. There is within her a presentiment of a life really deserving the name. One day she will have to obey it, without pausing to think. She knows that she will die of it, but she also knows that she can forget this knowledge when the time comes. Knows that death must come upon her unawares.

Sometimes I think that I would need all the other people in the world to make myself complete. There you see the madness of it.

What I see, Kleist, is need.

The woman is suffering, Kleist does not doubt it in the least, but women as a sex are born for suffering. She will adjust, even if—this much he will grant her—it will be harder for her than for most. In this way she resembles his sister. But he tells himself: She is provided for, whatever that may mean; she is not compelled to concentrate her thoughts on the most trivial demands of everyday life. It seems to him a kind of advantage that she has no choice in the matter. As a woman she is not placed under the law of having to achieve everything or to regard everything as nothing.

Kleist reckons up the number of countries he knows. It has become a compulsion for him to do so. He has learned that conditions in these countries run counter to his needs. With the best will in the world and a timid trust he has tried them out, and rejected them only against his will.

The sense of relief when he abandoned his hope for an earthly existence in any way corresponding to his needs.

Unlivable life. No place on earth.

Sometimes he can feel the distorted rotation of the spherical earth deep down inside his bones. One day he will be catapulted over the edge of this confining little sphere, he can already sense the wind rising. Whereas this woman here, improbable as it may seem, could even yet find her lover, an unpretentious little home in which she can gather children about her and forget the melancholy caprices of her youth.

Do you believe, Günderrode, that every human being has one secret he cannot tell anyone?

Yes, says Günderrode. In these times? Yes.

She had her answer all ready.

They stop and turn toward each other. Each of them sees the sky behind the other's head. The pale blue of late afternoon, little processions of clouds. They examine each other candidly, without reserve. Naked gazes. Self-abandonment, a tentative experiment. Smiles, first hers, then his, ironical. Let's pretend it's a game even if it's deadly earnest. You know it, I know it too. Don't come too close. Don't stay too far away. Conceal yourself. Reveal yourself. Forget what you know. Remember it. Masks fall away, superincrustations, scabs, varnish. The bare skin. Undisguised features. So that's my face. This is yours. Different down to the ground, alike from the ground up. Woman. Man. Untenable words. We two, each imprisoned in his sex. That touching we desire so infinitely does not exist. It was killed along with us. We should have to invent it.

It offers itself to us in dreams, disfigured, horrible, grotesque. The fear in the pale morning light, after one wakes up so early. We remain unknowable to each other, unapproachable, craving disguises. The names of strangers in which we wrap ourselves. The cry of lament forced back into the throat. Grieving is forbidden, for what losses have we suffered?

I am not I. You are not you. Who is "we"?

We are very alone. Insane diagrams which send us onto that eccentric path. Following the man one loves dressed in man's clothing. To practice a trade: a form of camouflage, first of all a camouflage from ourselves. Even if we are prepared to die, the wounds which people are forced to inflict on us still hurt. The pressure of the iron plates, as they move nearer in order to crush us or force us to the very edge, gradually takes our breath away. Short of breath, full of dread, we must go on speaking, that we know. As we know that no one hears us. And that they must all defend themselves against us: after all, what would become of them if they did not? They would end up where we are—and who could wish that on them, when we ourselves cannot wish to be where we are. When we cannot change the facts. When we love each other, hate each other.

That time should bring forth our desire, but not that which we desire most.

The repressed passions.

We are not worthy of that which we long for.

We must understand that longing needs no justification.

Time seems to be trying to bring about a new order of

things, and we will experience no part of it except the overthrow of the old.

To think that we may be understood by beings who have not yet been born.

The struggle to maintain one's self-control and proper deportment. As if, in the end, what we do or fail to do had some meaning.

Now the river is on the left, they are heading back toward the village. The sun is hanging low in the sky but it is still warm. A beautiful evening. Günderrode is breathing easily, Kleist no longer feels at all weak.

Soon he will return home, beneath the paler sky stretched taut above the towers of the castle, the roofs of the government buildings, among which he will walk back and forth along streets of methodical straightness; he can already see himself wearing a different kind of clothing, a different disguise. Sometimes, among strangers on the street, after hours of waiting in a dusty anteroom working on official documents, in the course of a conversation of no import whatever, he will be seized by a wicked desire to shriek. He will grit his teeth, clench his fists, suppress the impulse, and after a moment dry the sweat from his forehead. He is unlikely to think of a poet named Tian and will no doubt have forgotten his resolution to read her work. Only a rumor of her death will reach him and will touch him in a strange, remote way, while he, bound to his own shackles, employs heartrending maneuvers in the attempt to conceal the fact that he is having another breakdown; most sincerely and humbly grateful for a favor which was bound to destroy him, apologizing for the persistent sickly condition of his under-body, which corrodes his soul and makes him, in the strangest way, anxious during all those professional deal-ings to which he still has the good fortune to be sum-moned. So that, to his most heartfelt distress, he proves incapable of undertaking them any longer. He will not know the words which, at this very time, Günderrode is writing to the man she loves: Ours is a sad fate. I envy the rivers which merge. Death is better than such a life as this.

Now, Kleist, tell me about your play.

I believe that you are familiar with it.

Not about that one. About the one no one knows, not even yourself.

Since Wieland, she is the first person who has wanted to know about the *Guiscard*, which Kleist is trying to forget. Why is he resisting? Why is he refusing to supply a simple piece of information.

The questions you ask, Günderrode!

She has learned, she says, to tell the difference between sources of genuine pain and those which are not genuine, and then to take no account of the factitious ones, either in herself or in others.

She is calling his taciturnity factitious? Kleist is almost amused.

No, she is calling it unnecessary.

But I find it impossible to talk about certain things.

We'll see about that. She does not believe that he was

compelled to give up this work, which meant so much to him, for no reason. He may think her importunate, but she has a burning interest in the reason.

He has wanted someone to take these liberties.

She cannot believe the cause to have been a simple setback or failure. Only people without talent finished everything they started. Many surrenders merely demonstrated the strength of the resistance which had preceded them. In some cases, a project was bound to fail even though it was qualified for success in every way.

What cases, says Kleist.

No form can be found in which to cast an insoluble problem.

You amaze me.

You were thinking: So clever, considering she's only a woman.

Resentment, from you?

Dear Kleist, she says, people have been using that line from the beginning of time. They start early on, forbidding us to be unhappy about our sufferings, which are all imaginary. By the age of seventeen we must have accepted our fate, which is a man, and must learn and accept the penalty should we behave so improbably as to resist. How often I have wanted to be a man, longed for the real wounds to which you men expose yourselves!

Don't you see how our masculine duty to act is by nature something that cannot be fulfilled, that we can only act wrongly or not at all! Whereas at least you are free to do as you like within the realm of ideas, which has been appointed to you.

Ideas that lead nowhere. So we, too, help to divide humanity into doers and thinkers. Don't we perceive how the acts of those who usurp the right to take action involve less and less reflection, fewer scruples? How the poetry of those who fail to act corresponds more and more to the aims of those who take action? Must we who are unable to accommodate ourselves to any practical activity not fear that we may become members of that effeminate race of eternal whiners, incapable of the slightest concession to the demands that everyday affairs impose on everyone, and obstinately laying claim to a privilege which no one on earth can live up to: to act and at the same time to remain ourselves?

Who is speaking?

Now Kleist knows: he will go to Prussia, accept a civil-service post, and do his best to live up to the responsibilities it entails. Show the woman whom she is dealing with.

But just think, Günderrode: nowadays if we insist on the satisfaction of the most modest needs—something we consider indispensable—we come into discredit and are accused of wanting all or nothing. That's the pass things have come to. Step by step we're moving backwards.

That may be, but it does not excuse us anything. Tell me: do you live without any hidden guarantees? Without the secret hope that those who live after you will have some use for you even if your contemporaries can get along perfectly well without you? And yet don't you at the same time thirst for fame right now, in the present?

Say no more.

The man depends on makeshift expedients, fully expecting that they will collapse. Prepared for the fact that he will achieve neither the one nor the other ambition, but will simply fail. That he will remain inconsequential, a figure of marginal importance. One day, when his fervent efforts to find something to hold on to in the existing orders of the world have become meaningless; when he goes about among men unrecognized, sick with the humiliations which doubtless lie in store for him, and meeting with no response in that area which is most essential to him: only then will he claim the right to his sufferings, and at the same time the right to end them. That incomparable feeling when all the cords that bind you tear.

You are drifting away from me, Günderrode. Where?

You will not permit me to keep silent?

They remain standing there, she leaning against a willow tree. They gaze across the river. Shortly before its final descent, the sun is rolling fiery-red above the horizon, along the edge of the plateau on the other side. In a few minutes they see it disappear. Now there is no more need to think, no more need to speak.

What were we talking about?

We were talking about your play. You were going to explain it to me.

Explain! Now he feels he wants to.

A man, he hears himself say, at the height of his fame and his power, Robert Guiscard, Duke of Normandy and commander of the Norman army, must combat the plague which is decimating his men and which he himself is carrying inside his own body.

And he refuses to acknowledge it?

He deceives the army, which could not be controlled by a sick leader. Scorns all his solemn oaths that he will not tend the plague victims himself.

Just like Napoleon at Acre, says Günderrode. —Is she smiling?

That monster, says Kleist. Who believes he leads a charmed life and is proof against all attack.

And in fact actually has been up until now—unlike your Guiscard.

Günderrode! Guiscard, a man all of a piece, governed by his own will!

As Napoleon by his.

That madman! Devoured by his craving to dominate. Whereas Guiscard dominates himself for a purpose which transcends himself: to erect the kingdom of the Normans on Greek soil.

By what right does he claim to do this?

He is guided by a prophecy. He waits outside Constantinople, incapable of retreating. He has staked everything on this throw of the dice, burned all his bridges behind him. Don't you understand what that means?

Why is she keeping silent?

She wants to know about the prophecy.

It would have played a part in the action. It was prophesied to the historical Guiscard—who died on Corfu—that his life would end in Jerusalem. Too late he learned that here, on Corfu, where he had thought himself safe, there once lay a city called Jerusalem. How cruelly the prophecy led him astray.

So he dies cursing the gods who played their little game with him? Or cursing himself for having trusted them rather than himself alone? Did he frivolously and sacrilegiously impute to their decree ends identical to his own? Was he guilty of presumption? Or did he esteem himself too lightly?

That's just it, says Kleist. Who can possibly know?

In a few minutes the woman understands something which took him years: the fact that he had worn himself out trying to achieve the impossible. A man as closely bound to the laws of the Ancients as to those of his own day, and who is equally indebted to himself and to the treachery of the gods for effecting his downfall: the drama has not yet created a form for a hero such as this. But above all, as he now sees clearly: it is an insoluble task to desire to expose one's worst enemy and oneself at the same time. The subject of the play is colossal, to fail at it no disgrace.

He wants to divest himself of the incurable side of his nature.

I write only because I cannot help myself.

In order to prevent it from destroying him, Hölderlin made to the world the conciliatory proposal that the poet is mad.

Your proposal to the world, Günderrode? Hey, you all, love me?

And yours? Annihilate me?

Ah, Günderrode! To be able to be completely truthful with oneself.

It is not permitted us.

Often I think: What if the primal, ideal state created by nature, which we were compelled to destroy, could never lead to that second ideal state we envisage, via that organization which we have created for ourselves?

If we cease to hope, then that which we fear will surely come.

They walk along in silence. Günderrode draws this foreigner's attention to the play of color in the western sky, a rosy red and an apple green which appear nowhere else in nature. It is still light out, only the air is growing cooler. Günderrode draws her shawl together over her breast. She is calm. At this time of day she often wishes to be alone and dead to everything in the world, except for the one man whom she does not yet know and whom she will create for herself. She dismembers herself, making herself into three people, one of them a man. Love, provided that it is unconditional, can fuse the three separate people into one. The man beside her does not have this prospect before him. His work is the only point at which he can become one with himself: he dare not give it up for the sake of any human being. So he is doubly alone, doubly a captive. Things cannot go well for this man, regardless of whether he is a genius or only one among those many unhappy beings whom time spews out in its passage.

A line passes through Kleist's mind which he does not wish to quote to Günderrode: No woman has faith in her own strength. Through this woman, he thinks, her sex could achieve faith in itself. This exchange with her, which does not arouse him as a man, closely resembles a sensual intoxication.

She says, as if she had been thinking exactly the same thing: The moment we become aware of the present, it is already past. The consciousness of pleasure always lies in memory.

So I, too, thinks Kleist, will one day be a corpse in the thoughts of men? That is what they call immortality?

Between one time and another, she thinks, is a twilit region in which it is easy to go astray and get lost in some mysterious way. That does not terrify me. After all, life is taken out of our hands. But I do not have to exist forever. Does this mean that I am invulnerable?

For no reason she suddenly begins to laugh, first softly, then loudly and heartily. The laughter is infectious, and Kleist laughs, too. They have to hold on to each other in order not to fall down laughing. They will never be closer than they are at this moment.

If human beings, out of malice or incomprehension, indifference or fear, are forced to destroy certain members of their own species, then an incredible freedom falls to our lot who are destined to be destroyed. The freedom to love other people and not to hate ourselves.

To understand that we are a rough sketch—perhaps meant to be thrown away, perhaps to be taken up again: we have no control over that. It is worthy in a human being to laugh at this fact. Signed and signing. Assigned to perform a work which remains open, open like a wound.

What are they talking about now, or are they thinking?

We know too much. People will think we are raving mad. Our ineradicable faith that man is destined for self-perfection, a faith which runs counter to the spirit of this and every age. Is it an illusion?

The world does what comes most easily to it:

It keeps silent.

The light has changed. All objects, even the trees, are acute, glaring and piercing. From far off they hear voices; they are calling for Kleist. The coach to Mainz is about to leave. Günderrode motions to him to depart. Their leave-taking consists in a movement of the hand.

Now it is getting dark. The final glow on the river.

Simply go on, they think.

We know what is coming.

Translator's Notes

4 *"Winkel, on the Rhine . . . June 1804"*

It was in this small town in the Rhineland—traditionally on a tongue of land like that which Günderrode is here described as observing through the window—that the twenty-six-year-old poet Karoline von Günderrode (1780–1806) stabbed herself to death only two years after the events of this novella, when she was once again visiting the country estate of the merchant Joseph Merten. Here in Winkel, in July of 1806, she received word that the professor and comparative mythologist Friedrich Creuzer, a married man, had definitively broken off their relationship.

There is no proof that Günderrode ever met the drama-
tist Heinrich von Kleist (1777–1811)—who committed
suicide on the banks of the Wannsee only a few years
later, in November of 1811—either at Joseph Merten's
gathering for the literati of the Romantic movement or on
another occasion.

5 *"Dr. Wedekind"*
It was Dr. Wedekind (George Christian Wedekind) who
cared for Kleist after his physical and mental collapse in
France. Kleist, in abandoning his army career, broke with
the distinguished military traditions of his family. He had
failed in his efforts to fill a civil-service post; had abandoned his studies after coming to believe, on the basis of
Kant's *Critique of Pure Reason,* in the unattainability of
intellectual certitude; and he had broken his engagement
to a general's daughter. It was after these events and his
attempt to write the ambitious drama *Robert Guiscard*
that Kleist suffered a breakdown, destroyed the manuscript of the drama, and ended up in Mainz under the
care of Dr. Wedekind.

The "Schlegel translation" of *Hamlet* is one of a noted
series of Shakespeare translations into German made by
August Wilhelm Schlegel.

5 *"Worthy is sorrow to lie at the heart of man, and to be
your intimate friend, O Nature!"*
Günderrode is quoting from the *Hyperion* of Friedrich
Hölderlin (1770–1843), whom she greatly admired and to
whose verse her own is said to be akin. At this date, 1804,
"the crazed poet" Hölderlin had already suffered his first
bout of insanity; he would soon lapse completely into that

mentally-shrouded state which constituted the second half of his existence.

6 *"I ought to have stayed back at the convent"*
Like Kleist, Günderrode came from an impoverished noble family. While still in her teens, she was forced, because of family finances, to enter the Cronstetten-Hynspergische Evangelical Sisterhood in Frankfurt am Main. This was less a convent in the strict sense than a sanctuary for impoverished gentlewomen, and Günderrode retained sufficient freedom to pursue an active program of self-education as well as to become the object of the affections of three of the innovative intellectuals of her time—the Romantic poet Clemens Brentano, the jurist Friedrich Karl von Savigny, and Friedrich Creuzer. Nor did the religious life prevent her from publishing some of her poems in 1804 and 1805 under the pseudonym "Tian."

6 *"Savigny and Bettine"*
Friedrich Karl von Savigny (1779–1861) was a renowned German jurist, professor, and author of distinguished books on the law, who eventually reached the highest echelons of government. He frequented Romantic circles and married Kunigunde Brentano (here called by her nickname, Gunda), the sister of the more gifted Clemens and Bettine Brentano. He also maintained a long and loyal, if somewhat precarious, relationship with Karoline von Günderrode.

Bettine Brentano (later Bettine von Arnim; 1785–1859) was sister to the Romantic writer Clemens Brentano, and later wife to his friend and collaborator Achim von Arnim. She moved in Romantic circles and published several books of fiction in the form of letters ostensibly exchanged between herself and notable persons of her day, including Goethe. In 1840 she published *Die Günderode,* a free rendering of her correspondence with Günderrode (whom here she calls by her nickname, Lina). She remained devoted to Günderrode, whom she had first met while staying with F. K. von Savigny in Marburg not long before the events of the novella.

9   *"The mocking young Wieland"*
Christoph Martin Wieland (1733–1813), far from young at this stage, was an established figure in the world of German letters and had befriended Kleist during one of the newly fledged playwright's bouts of depression. Recognizing his genius, Wieland encouraged Kleist to complete his drama *Robert Guiscard,* which, after hearing a fragment, Wieland considered a work unparalleled in German literature.

9   *"The renowned Clemens Brentano, who, to Kleist's chagrin, retired with his young wife, Sophie Mereau, and another young couple, the Esenbecks"*
Clemens Brentano (1778–1842), a noted author and collector and adapter of folk songs during the Romantic period, wooed Sophie Mereau, a professor's wife and also a writer, until she divorced her husband to marry Brentano in 1803. She died in childbirth in 1806—the year of Günderrode's suicide. The child to whom, in the novella, she has just given birth is her and Brentano's first child, Joachim (Achim) Ariel, born May 1804, who died in June, shortly after the literary tea takes place.

Christian Nees von Esenbeck (1776–1858), a noted

German botanist, was married to one of Günderrode's closest friends, Lisette Mettingh.

11   *"His doomed struggle to write the accursed* Guiscard"
Kleist reputedly burned the manuscript of his drama *Robert Guiscard: Duke of the Normans* in 1803, in the midst of a devastating physical and mental collapse in Paris, which led to an attempt, alluded to later, to commit suicide by joining the forces of Napoleon—whom he detested—before the projected French invasion of England, in the hope of being shot by the English. In 1804, Kleist reconstructed one passage of the lost drama from memory. The plot of *Guiscard* is based on the life of the Norman duke (*d.* 1085), who sought to capture Byzantium for the Norman empire. Guiscard is dying, but tries to accomplish the task he has set for himself, in defiance of fate.

22   *"But the review in* Der Freimüthige"
In a letter dated May 31, 1804, Günderrode wrote to Savigny that it had become public knowledge that she was the author of the poems signed "Tian." She enclosed a censorious review written by a native of her own Frankfurt and signed "E.," published in the periodical *Der Freimüthige,* whose publisher, Kotzebue, was antagonistic to the Romantic writers, being, like Goethe, part of the old guard.

27   *"His Wilhelmine . . . Voss's* Luise"
Wilhelmine von Zenge was Kleist's fiancée until 1802, when he broke with her in a letter of farewell. Johann Heinrich Voss (1751–1826) was the author of *Luise: A Rural Poem in Three Idylls* (published in 1795), a popu-

lar work in the German classical style, characterized by harmonious metrics and tepid subject matter. It tells of the preparations for a wedding and ends with the couple's entrance into the bridal chamber.

47   *"Your hand, Savigny: does it still hurt?"*
This passage is based on a letter from Savigny to Günderrode dated December 14, 1803. Using a cipher language—as they often did—he refers to their stormy final separation and to an unnamed someone who slammed the coach door on his hand as they parted, leaving a lesion that the doctors diagnosed as a burn.

59   *"A few years ago I was standing with a certain young man . . . in the garden of the Leonhardi estate"*
It was on the Leonhardi estate, country seat of friends of Günderrode's, that in 1799 she first met and was attracted to Savigny. This description of the encounter corresponds to that found in one of her letters to him.

   The brother Savigny mentions is Günderrode's only brother, Hektor Wilhelm.

74   *"Thereupon Narcissus replies"*
This extract is from Günderrode's poem "Wandel und Treue" ("Change and Constancy"), first published in 1804 in her collection *Gedichte und Phantasien*.

81   *"In other words, man, like Ixion, is damned to trundle a wheel up a mountain"*
The Ixion image is from one of Kleist's letters. In it, Kleist combines the tale of Sisyphus with that of Ixion,

who was attached to a fiery wheel for his attempt to seduce Hera while accepting the hospitality of Zeus.

83 *"Goethe's Tasso . . . the Privy Councilor of Weimar"*
The Privy Councilor of Weimar is, of course, Goethe, who for many years held a high cabinet post under Duke Karl August of Saxe-Weimar. Goethe's verse drama *Torquato Tasso* (first published in 1790) deals with the life of the famous Italian poet after the great success of his work *La Gerusalemme liberata,* or more generally, with the conflict between the artist and the statesman or the man of affairs. In *Tasso,* Leonora Sanvitale, a figure who is cited later in Kleist's conversation with Günderrode, expresses her regret that artist and statesman could not have been molded by Nature into a single man.

87 *"Sweet May, young man of blossoms"*
The original German of this poem of Brentano's is from the period of his *Gedichte* (1804–1815).

97 *"To give birth to what slays me"*
This is a line from a poem by Günderrode, "Die Einzige," expressing the unconditional and fatal—to herself—nature of her love for Creuzer.

103 *"You ardent red"*
This is a line from Günderrode's poem "Hochroth"—found among her posthumous papers—which reflects the intensity of her experience of love.

109 *"Following the man one loves dressed in man's clothing"*
During the time of her involvement with Creuzer,

Günderrode considered several desperate moves, including that of donning men's clothing so that she could be near him at the university. Günderrode frequently experienced herself as a man—the result of her very modern confusion over sexual roles.

III *"Ours is a sad fate"*
This is from a fragment of a letter written by Günderrode to Friedrich Creuzer in April 1806, three months before their relationship ended and she killed herself.

A MODEL CHILDHOOD

'This is a powerful book, a most extraordinary testament ... it is her vision of the fundamental strangeness of what seemed at the time a fairly ordinary childhood, in the bosom of a normal Nazi family in Landsberg, which makes Christa Wolf's narrative so moving, so convincing'
– *The Times*

In 1933 four-year-old Nelly lives in Landsberg. Her family believes in Hitler's new order: her father joins the party, and she, as a matter of course, joins the Nazi youth organisations. In school Nelly learns of racial purity and the Jewish threat, and when the local synagogue burns, she feels not pity, only fear of an alien race. No voice of objection is raised, not even when the euthanasia programme dooms Nelly's simple-minded Aunt Dottie. It is only much later, when her family flees westward before the advancing Russian army, that Nelly, now in her teens, tries to come to terms with the shattering of the fundamental values of her childhood. This great novel is a plea to remember and to learn from the past.

VIRAGO MODERN CLASSICS

The first Virago Modern Classic, *Frost in May* by Antonia White, was published in 1978. It launched a list dedicated to the celebration of women writers and to the rediscovery and reprinting of their works. Its aim was, and is, to demonstrate the existence of a female tradition in fiction which is both enriching and enjoyable, and to broaden the sometimes narrow academic definition of a 'classic' which has often led to the neglect of a large number of interesting secondary works of fiction. In calling the series 'Modern Classics' we do not necessarily mean 'great' — although this is often the case. Published with new critical and biographical introductions, books are chosen for many reasons: sometimes for their importance in literary history; sometimes because they illuminate particular aspects of women's lives, both personal and public. They may be classics of comedy or storytelling; their interest can be historical, feminist, political or literary.

Initially the Virago Modern Classics concentrated on English novels and short stories published in the early decades of this century. As the series has grown it has broadened to include works of fiction from different centuries, different countries, cultures and literary traditions, many of which have been suggested by our readers.